DATE DUE 10/01

NOV 0 8 '01			
JAN 07 '02			
FEB 1 9 '02			
AP 2 4 '02			
SE 0 4 03			
JA 2 8 '04			
GAYLORD			PRINTED IN U.S.A.

An Empire of Women

KAREN SHEPARD

An Empire of Women

WHEELER
PUBLISHING, INC.
ROCKLAND, MA

★ AN AMERICAN COMPANY ★

Published in Large Print by arrangement with G.P. Putnam's Sons, a member of Penguin Putnam Inc., in the United States and Canada.

Wheeler Large Print Book Series.

Set in 16 pt Plantin.

Library of Congress Cataloging-in-Publication Data

Shepard, Karen.
    An empire of women / Karen Shepard.
       p. (large print) cm.(Wheeler large print book series)
    ISBN 1-58724-077-7 (hardcover)
    1. Asian American women—Fiction. 2. Mothers and daughters—Fiction. 3. Virginia—Fiction. 4. Large type books. I. Title. II. Series

[PS3569.H39388 E47   2001]
813'.6—dc21
                                               2001026354
                                                   CIP

For Jim

Prologue

They were three women fighting over a child who belonged, really, to none of them. The women preferred not to be grouped together in any way, not even in an introductory sentence. But there was no avoiding it.

Celine Arneaux was the grandmother, six days shy of seventy-five years old. Her favorite alcohol was sherry. Her favorite drink was green tea in a Communist Chinese mug, enamel, with a lid, with perhaps a quick color drawing of a cherry blossom or sparrow around its width. She ate quickly, in the manner of someone who had spent years with multiple siblings, or in prison, though she had experienced neither. She was the only child of a Chinese merchant's daughter and a French surgeon. Born in Shanghai on July 14, 1915, she had lived in China until she was twelve, then Paris until 1939, when she left her parents for an apartment in New York and a cabin in Virginia. Since 1978, she had been back in Paris in a sprawling apartment with a view of a small, three-sided park. She would not admit how much she missed the States.

She was a famous photographer. She still washed her hands as if having just worked with chemicals. Her nails were short, not bitten. When she liked you a lot, she invited you to sit beside her while she opened her mail.

At nearly seventy-five, she weighed the same one hundred and thirty pounds that she had weighed as a twenty-year-old. She was five-foot-nine; five-ten in the Bally shoes she'd always been able to afford, and had first had purchased for her at the opening day—spring 1928—of the Bally store on Boulevard de la Madeleine. She can still visualize the façade designed by Mallet-Stevens. She was too tall for an Asian woman, and her Chinese friends were polite and pretended not to notice.

She was even more well known in China than she was in the States. She visited there at least twice a year. She was vocal in her support of the Chinese Government. She liked to refer to spoiled American children with some irony as "Capitalist running dogs." When asked why she didn't just live in China, she would shake her head and say she could do more good from outside China. It was best, she said, to have one foot in each place. The Tien An Men massacre had shaken her more than she liked to admit. She had cried for days. But by now, a year after the fact, she had talked herself back into possible explanations for the Government's actions.

When someone's behavior pained her, she pursed her whole face, like a disappointed dog.

Her favorite breeds were vizslas and pugs, though she had never owned either, preferring, when she was a child, to entice the stray cats to the back door with plates of leftovers hand-prepared by her family chef.

She had more money than almost any other photographer of her generation, and had always thought she would. Combined with her family money, the money from the photographs made quite a sum. She had been known to say, "I happen to have millions." Giving money to strangers bothered her less than giving it to her daughter or granddaughter.

Her pregnancy had been trouble-free, but her labor and delivery so agonized that she still hadn't fully forgiven her daughter. The Chinese painter with whom she had conceived the baby had been a small, kind man with skin the color of white peaches. He had gone back to China, to his beautiful garden city, to his Old Master teachers, to his arranged marriage. She'd found out she was pregnant a month after he left. She didn't tell him about their daughter. She didn't answer his letters, and soon they stopped coming. She did not allow herself images of what her life with him might've been. Occasionally, she saw his hands, or the curve of his lashes. Occasionally, she felt the press of his lips against her closed eyes. "These eyes," he would say to her.

She'd been hospitalized only one other time: at fifteen, for surgery to remove three-quarters of a tubercular lung. Her father had performed the operation. He had brought

3

her bowls of her favorite fruits, black cherries and lichees, each day for the month she had had to stay in the hospital. Eleven years later, in November of 1941, her father had been invited by the German occupiers to attend their conference on tuberculosis. He had found a way to refuse without offending anyone.

She wore her hair short, cropped like a man's; the shorter layers swept just above her ears and seemed to hold their shape through sheer will. She didn't use hairspray. She didn't use conditioner.

She never brought gifts when she visited friends, though she routinely chided others for failing to do so. She preferred food to flowers, especially items that she would never think of buying for herself, like toasted sesame sticks or coconut macaroons.

She hadn't taken a single image in over twelve years, and the next day's trip to the cabin in Virginia where all the photographs were made had given her three days of stomachaches and headaches, for which she refused to take any medicine, because she was, in general, the kind of woman who didn't take medicine.

Cameron Arneaux, born in 1965, was the subject of her grandmother's photographs. Their birthdays were three days apart, and Cameron had spent much of her life complaining about the burden of having to share. She would be twenty-five this year, and she would rather have been spending the day in a tub surrounded by vanilla candles and reading a magazine, a wet washcloth draped across her breasts.

Her carriage and poise inspired envy. She was an eighth French, three-eighths Chinese and half Japanese. Her breasts were large enough to be noticed by women, but small enough not to require a bra. Her hips were practically curveless, her collarbone as pronounced as a ballerina's. Her elbows were surprisingly dry, like an elephant's. She used a discount-brand moisturizer and never washed her face. She was allergic to perfume and always told the hairdresser not to dry or style her hair. Her hair was the most Asian thing about her. Children sitting next to her on the bus reached over to touch it.

She had lost her virginity at sixteen to a thirty-one-year-old man she had picked up at a club. She'd thought of it as a trial run for the next guy, the guy she would really love. The sheets involved had had wild animals all over them, the color of an African veldt during the dry season. In high school and college she had had unprotected sex often, flirting with images of babies. She had never known her father, a Japanese man who'd been Celine's assistant one summer. Her mother and grandmother had told her he'd returned to Japan; they didn't know where to find him. She'd never had an abortion, but most of her friends had. She got sick easily and took longer than most to get well. She had asthma. She had chronic

5

headaches. She sucked her thumb until she was ten.

By the time she was seven, she would read for hours on end by herself. The parents of her friends found it disconcerting. Her favorite books involved real-life survivor stories from World War II.

She liked to dance, but didn't like dance parties. When she did dance, people around her invariably began imitating her, sometimes without realizing it. She liked partner dancing and wished she were better at it. She shopped at the secondhand clothing stores run by East Side private girls' schools or at the fifty-percent-off sales at a French designer's small boutique on Prince Street. Her friends thought she was frugal. Her Visa bills were routinely over a thousand dollars. The highest one had been four thousand. She had grown tired, years ago, of thanking her mother for getting Celine to put aside a large part of her money for Cameron's future. Every so often, it bothered her that she depended on that money. It didn't bother her enough to make her do anything about it.

She forgot to eat for days, except when working on a portrait. When she worked, she ate foods that she could eat quickly: Shredded Wheat out of the box, peanuts, Fuji apples and Red Globe grapes. Her paints often had crumbs in them. She told people her secret was eight glasses of water a day, but she barely drank one. Ginger ale was her favorite soda. She drank tea, but enjoyed the image of herself drinking tea much more than the tea itself. When she wanted to get drunk, she drank margaritas with salt through a straw.

Her palette included no pastels. Sometimes she arranged her wedding bouquet in her mind.

Two months earlier, she'd gotten her MFA in painting from NYU. Her grandmother had paid for it. She had not been close to any of her professors. She had not offended any of them. Everyone knew the photographs. Only her closest friends knew she had money. Everyone knew that she thought she was almost as famous as her grandmother. Three books, at ages one, six and twelve; three internationally recognized shows. She kept the books in a drawer under her bed. She had overheard the other graduate students agreeing among themselves that she wasn't as beautiful in real life as in the photos.

Her favorite article of clothing was a pair of black bike shorts. She didn't bike. She didn't do any regular exercise, except for the summer after her first year at Vassar, when she'd gone to three hours of aerobics every day, jogging to and from class to her apartment. She'd closed her eyes for the first and the last block of the run.

She'd gained fifty pounds freshman year, and had lost sixty that summer. There were still faint silvery stretch marks on her upper thighs and lower abdomen. Her stomach had never been flat. She worried that her forehead was too broad. She didn't share anxieties with anyone except for her best friend from graduate school, an exchange student from Beijing. She owned only one mirror, but she stood in front of it often.

She lived in Manhattan on the fifth floor of 609 West 112th Street, across the street from a progressive elementary school and next to a welfare hotel. She visited her mother infrequently. One of her favorite activities was folding her clothes. She had worked during high school vacations at a Benetton store. For Christmas, she had given her fellow employees tiny boxes of Godiva chocolates. She liked laundry and clean dishes. She liked throwing bag after bag of garbage down the garbage chute in her building. She preferred walking to riding the subway, though she did buy her tokens in ten-packs. As she walked, she composed letters she would never put down on paper. It embarrassed her to go to movies or restaurants alone, but walking into a bar by herself gave her a small thrill. In her high school yearbook, the first photograph was a two-page spread of her working as a life model for a painting class. She shared her senior page with a girl she hadn't talked to since graduation. She chose three quotes for the page: the definition of pentimento from Lillian Hellman's *Pentimento*; an anonymous quote written in French, without a translation; and this excerpt from an article in *The Times-Picayune*: "She said she turned him in to the police because she loved him. If she hadn't, he probably never would have been caught.

8

She testified she hoped he would get help. But it didn't turn out the way she expected." She spelled Picayune "Piciun."

Men thought that going out with her would be more magical than it actually turned out to be. She had never met a man who she thought was smarter than she was.

She once slapped the hand of a five-year-old just so she could comfort him. It was the thing she was most ashamed of.

$\mathcal{S}$umin Arneaux thought that she loved animals but in reality didn't even like them. She did like wooden toys, especially those with moveable parts. She liked stickers and decorative notecards. She liked blank books.

She expected racism from most people.

She was the result of her mother's affair with a visiting Chinese painter in New York. She had been born in 1942, three years after Celine had moved to the States. She'd had Cameron at twenty-three; Celine had had Sumin at twenty-seven. Sumin was secretly and irrationally proud of having done something at an earlier age than her mother.

She spent the summer of 1974 learning how to sail on Long Island Sound and hadn't sailed since. She had lived in New York her whole life, but didn't think of it as home. She fantasized about moving to Santa Fe. She made appointments she didn't keep with real-estate agents there.

For the last five years, she had lived in Brooklyn with Grady Baxter, a Sinophile and journalist almost as wealthy and nearly as old as Celine. He had a cat named China whom Sumin found vaguely repulsive. He had once told Sumin that her name sounded like a spice.

She didn't believe in marriage.

She had already let her daughter know that when the time came she didn't want to be called Grandma. One of her favorite things about being a mother had been the excuse it gave her to do non-adult activities. By the time Cam was five, Sumin was taking her to the Central Park carousel once a week. She rode when Cameron wouldn't. She took Cam to see *Sounder, The Sound of Music*, and *The Aristocats*. Also, a film festival of Japanese samurai movies. And *Lenny*. And *Walking Tall*.

She used only comforters on her beds, never top sheets. She had a sign at her door asking you to please take off your shoes. She carried Sucrets throat lozenges in her purse. During the seventies she wore a pair of bell-bottom jeans with embroidered red, white and blue stars all over them. She liked hats. When she was depressed, she rearranged furniture.

She cooked Peking Duck and made Almond Junket. She liked tapioca pudding and Postum. She bought, and never used, chopped walnuts. She made elaborate Chinese dinners look as easy as TV dinners.

People often thought that she was alcoholic, but she wasn't.

As a way to keep track of her aging, she would pull at the skin on the back of her hand and see how long it took to return to place. She was forty-eight, but said she might as well be fifty. She had no close women friends. She and Grady periodically had conversations, explicit and implicit, about the pain of deceit versus the erotic appeal of deceit.

She slept late in the mornings and stayed up late at night. She kept a glass mug on her kitchen counter for used tea bags. She carried a nail clipper on her key ring. She had a small blue birthmark at the base of her spine. Her hair had yet to turn grey. She owned a rowing machine and a sit-up board, and used them, but stopped once she broke a sweat. She owned multiple pairs of hospital slippers she stole when Cameron had a broken wrist.

She liked incense coils. She stuck them in the houseplants. She used Tiger Balm for headaches. She liked the smell so much that sometimes she dabbed some under her nose when not feeling ill. At her mother's insistence, she took Chinese lessons—Mandarin and Cantonese—from the time she was five, for ten years. She didn't speak either now. She wore sunglasses indoors. Large groups made her nervous. The thought of public speaking made her break out. She often said the birth of her daughter was the most important moment of her life. She had a real way with children who weren't her own.

She'd never had health insurance. She went from being supported by her mother to being supported by Grady. She divided her money into three different wallets, all of which she carried in the same purse. She had been mugged twice. She never used sunscreen. She sunbathed with a towel over her face. The message on her answering machine sounded angry even though she didn't mean it to.

She was five-foot-three and had a row of vaccination scars down each arm. Almost all shoe styles were painful for her to wear. She bought velvet stretch leggings and matching socks from street vendors. She bought only paperbacks. When she gave them as gifts, she inscribed them. She liked outdoor showers. She had made, over the course of Cameron's life, multiple scrapbooks and albums, for herself.

She sometimes wished to be a poet. She read with a pink highlighter. For the last few days, she had been reading *Child of Mine: Writers Talk About the First Year of Motherhood*. The prospect of the drive to the cabin with her daughter thrilled her, but the prospect of the week at the cabin itself had created a rash across her chest and neck. To comfort herself, she made Kahlua milkshakes and drank them without a straw.

The next day, the three women would travel to Virginia, where all of the photographs were made. The first visit in twelve years. A joint birthday party for Cameron and Celine, and a return to the cabin for the purposes of a retrospective article written by Grady.

They would also need to make a decision about Alice Shen, a six-year-old mainland Chinese girl, belonging to none of them. She was now the fourth female in the group, and her future was theirs to decide.

Three Women

A TALL WOMAN in traditional Chinese dress on the left; a much shorter, younger woman on the right; a baby between them. All three of them have black, black hair.

It's unclear which woman the baby belongs to. The woman on the right holds her in a way that suggests an offering, and the taller woman circles the baby's forearm with her hand.

The baby holds her feet up for the camera, splaying excessively long toes as if showing them off.

Both women look at the baby. The baby looks at the camera. Her expression cannot be described as happy. It communicates a combination of anxiety and resignation.

The background is unremarkable.

Sunday

Sumin and Cameron were back on the entrance ramp before they realized Alice wasn't in the car. Cam cursed, threw the Volkswagen into reverse and started backing up. Her silver bracelets jangled.

Mother and daughter were on Interstate 81, somewhere in Pennsylvania. Sumin realized that if it came to talking to authorities, it would sound bad that they didn't know exactly where in Pennsylvania they were. She tried to visualize the exit number.

The car was still traveling in reverse. Sumin held on to the dash and looked straight ahead. *This* seemed unnecessary, she said to her daughter. There were horns. She avoided looking at the other drivers.

Cam swerved to avoid a pickup. She took a breath. "Mother," she began. She used the term only when particularly annoyed.

"Don't talk," Sumin said.

"Shut up," her daughter replied.

The Texaco station was just past the intersection. Cam looked both ways and drove through the red light. A man in a station wagon opposite them shook his finger.

"All I'm saying," Sumin continued, "is that if it were me driving..."

Cam turned in to the station. "If it were you driving, Alice would've ended up living with the gas station owner, his wife and their fourteen kids."

Alice was standing next to the pump. It was where the car had been when she'd gone to the bathroom. She was wearing red culottes and a red-and-white-striped T-shirt. Her plastic sandals were orange. Except for her sandals, she matched the colors of the Texaco sign. She was short for her age, and her straight black hair that hung to the middle of her back made her seem even shorter. Sumin found her faith touching and vaguely frightening. Cam beeped the horn to get the girl's attention and then waved and smiled at her.

How in God's name was Cam going to raise this six-year-old?

Alice didn't move as they pulled up. She allowed herself to be hugged and apologized to and walked back to the car.

Sumin turned to her and said, "Let's talk about what to do if this happens again."

This wasn't going to happen again, Cam told Alice, because from now on, when she needed to go to the bathroom, someone would always go with her. Cam gave her mother a look.

"Oh no," Sumin said. "You're not pinning this on me. She asked where the bathroom was; I told her."

Cam lowered her voice. "She's six," she said to her mother.

"My point exactly," Sumin responded. Then she leaned closer to Cam and added in a stage whisper, "She can hear you. It's a Volkswagen Bug."

"Ha," Alice said.

Sumin scrunched her nose at her.

Cam looked at Alice in the rearview mirror. "Whatever," she said. "Just don't worry. This won't happen again, okay?"

The girl looked back and forth at them, moving just her eyes rather than her whole head. She patted Cam on the shoulder. "I'm okay," she said. "I'm okay."

Sumin turned back around and smiled. It felt good to have an ally; unfamiliar and pleasant.

❧

A story I told Alice over the telephone, which she asked me to tell her again, less than a week later—*Please, Celine, just once more:* The silk store in Shanghai that I had to beg my mother to let me visit. *Don't be silly,* she would say. *We don't go out for dressmaking; they come to us.* But once, she relented. Broad, lacquered counters covered in white felt. The store employed only male attendants with manicured nails so as not to damage the silks. Even as a nine-year-old, I was struck dumb with appreciation for a place in which everything was so smooth, as if buffed to a high gloss. How did they get their nails like that? What would it feel like to lie between those bolts and bolts of silk?

Alice laughed with pleasure at the phrase: *bolts and bolts of silk.*

Now at Charles de Gaulle, however many years later, I sat in despair at the prospect of travel. Hours to Washington, D.C.; more hours in the car to the cabin in Virginia. Airports used to be like the theater. Men wore suits. Women wore hats and gloves. Theater in Paris in the thirties with my father. What I looked forward to most was dressing up, standing at the bar for the long intermission, dining afterwards at L'Aiglon or Fouquet's. We always sat at one particular banquette at L'Aiglon. We sat side by side with a view of the other diners. Now I suffered families in sweatsuits. Glossy horrible things with rescue-vehicle colors.

I chose a chair close to the boarding gate, far from an American family with three boys. I was wearing Thai silk—purple, hand-embroidered in golden thread. I smoothed the tunic under me as I sat. My chair was plastic, uncomfortable. A distasteful odor circulated.

I had packed the other silks last. The beige blouse, the chocolate pants would wrinkle. White tissue paper from the bedroom closet, folded into the silks, was the only way to prevent it. I'd taught Cam this.

I taught my granddaughter everything. Cam had had everything.

Memories floated through me like manta rays. Unexpected, they glided up, constant reminders of how much the present owed the past.

The first floor of the marketplace a "bad girl"

in school had taken me to one day after I moved to Paris. Satin shoes tattered from dancing, artificial flowers, stained silk dresses, torn lace skirts, all bought by the poorest girls as costumes. Literal-minded interviewers made the place the seed of my tendency to costume Cam. It was the sort of simpleminded connection at which interviewers excelled.

An idiot Englishman with his public school imagination connected the theatricality of my shots to Hill and Adamson's work of the 1840s: calotypes of friends dressed up in armor or as monks, illustrating passages from the novels of Sir Walter Scott.

A passage from that Greek fellow's review of *Six* in *The New York Times* which I could still quote: "The intimate, familial, biological connection between photographer and child is palpable—is, in fact, the essential aspect of their emotional content." (Finally a moment of insight in a review: I was Cameron's essential aspect. And she mine.)

I'd agreed too quickly to this article. Who knew what this Grady wanted out of the piece? He'd been living with Sumin for years; how serious a journalist could he be? Nothing he had said during the two times I had met him had convinced me of any intelligence. And who wanted to resurrect the Cam photographs and all that came with them? Wasn't that why I'd moved back to Paris? Hadn't I said that all that was finished? Cameron until the age of twelve had been a mystery, a puzzle. After twelve, something happened to the most captivating of girls. They became the solution to the equation, not the equation itself.

There was general public uproar at my decision. There were articles about what might entice me back to Cam. There were retrospectives lamenting what might've been. Cam seemed, as usual, unperturbed. As if she hadn't given the future of our photos any thought at all. I barely remembered Sumin's reaction. Something filled with nervousness, I was sure.

And it was only *Aperture*.

Still, a whole issue. I'd never been able to turn down any kind of sustained attention.

A time to take stock. This would-be interviewer's intended enticement. He was out of his depth, and he was the one with whom I would have to deal.

I had announced to him that I was too old to regret anything. I had lived beyond the age of regret. And now, sitting on my grey plastic chair, I thought, isn't that what we spend our lives doing, simply trying to get away with it all?

It was too warm in the airport's waiting area. Other travelers' noises made me warmer. I loosened my scarf. At least I'd been successful in resisting the magazine's offer for one of their people to accompany me on the trip. Even up until last night, whoever they had assigned had persisted. He had rung twice. Was I sure I didn't want his help? It would give him a chance to meet me; he was an admirer. He was also doing the background work on the article.

Taking the trip together would give us a chance to fill in some blanks. It had been exactly the wrong thing to say. I closed my eyes. I smoothed my silk tunic across my legs again.

And there was the child, with the Lewis Carroll name. Cam was not up to the task. I had told her as much on numerous occasions over the last six months. She shouldn't have agreed to be the girl's guardian in the first place. The girl belonged back in China with her mother, not in America. I'd told Cam this as well. I'd told her that I had started making the arrangements with my contacts in the Chinese government; she would understand, in time, that this was the only way. Cam had asked me to stop arranging; she would bring the girl to the cabin; I could see them together. She could show me that this was what her life had needed; this was what she had been made to do.

Please, I'd said. But I'd agreed, charmed by the heat of her attention. And, more surprisingly, pleased at the thought of a child in the cabin after all those years.

When I developed the first pictures of Cam, Yeats rang in my head. "Leda and the Swan," and the last lines of "Her Triumph": "And now we stare astonished at the sea, / And a miraculous strange bird shrieks at us." And my own words, from an early interview in Lucien Vogel's *Vu*, up until then hollow: The intensity with which a subject is grasped is what makes for beauty in art.

*B*ack on the interstate, in the middle of Cam and Sumin's discussion about how Alice had been left in the first place, the little girl lay down across the backseat and fell asleep.

Cam whispered, "Now see what you've done."

Sumin stared at her daughter. "She's asleep."

"She does it when she's anxious," Cam said. "It's a thing."

The girl's seat belt was straining across her middle. Sumin thought about unbuckling it. "She's asleep," she said again. "How can it be a thing?"

Cam didn't answer, and they were both quiet for a few minutes. The Volkswagen vibrated as the speedometer climbed past sixty.

Sumin said, "Are you really going to keep her?"

"She's not a dog," Cam said. "If you say you're going to be responsible for someone, you do it. You don't just pass her off to someone else." Cam flipped her sun visor down, then flipped it back up again. Sumin couldn't figure out what her daughter was getting at.

She said, "All I'm saying is that sometimes the responsible thing is to admit you're not up to the task. Sometimes that's the best thing."

Cam didn't say anything.

Sumin went on, whispering. "Even if her father's nowhere to be found, her mother's not dead. It's not like she has no one."

Cam leaned forward over the wheel and talked quietly to the top of the dashboard. "She has no one here. In February, her mother had to go back to China—her student visa was up. If she could've stayed she would've. She wants Alice to be raised in the States. Guardianship is a way to do that. She's lived here since she was two as it is."

Sumin fiddled with one of her silver and turquoise rings. She shook her head. "I don't think you understand all this as well as you should. What does that mean? You have Alice forever, or Mom just drops in whenever she wants and whooshes her away?"

Cam took a breath. "We've been over all this," she said. "Her mother is my closest friend from graduate school. She wants to be with Alice. Permament moves to the States are not that easy for mainland Chinese. Study abroad, visits to see family, that's one thing. Staying, that's something different. It's not like she's just handing her daughter over." Here, she paused and looked at her mother.

Sumin stared back.

Cam went on. "It just isn't very likely the Chinese Government's going to agree to a permanent move anytime soon."

"And what will you do when that happens?" Sumin asked.

The question went unanswered.

Sumin shook her head. "It's all very bizarre. Isn't it pretty unusual that she brought the kid with her in the first place?"

Cam didn't answer.

Sumin went on. "How well do you know this mother anyway? *I've* never heard you talk about her." She reached into her handbag at her feet and rummaged around. "And what kind of name is Alice? She's from China."

Cam opened and closed her hands around the steering wheel. "She has a Chinese name; her mom just wanted her to fit in. To be like the other kids."

Again, Sumin felt like they weren't talking about what she thought they were. She said, "And what do you tell Alice about all this?" She glanced back at the sleeping girl.

"The truth," Cam said.

Sumin snorted. "What does the six-year-old make of that?" she asked.

Cam looked over her shoulder and changed lanes. "Six-year-olds can be pretty resilient," she said.

Sumin felt warm. "So, she's handling it okay?" she asked, annoyed her daughter had set up the implied parallel.

Cam looked straight ahead. "You know what?" she said. "I appreciate the concern; I do." She softened her tone. "But it really has nothing to do with you."

Whether it was the kindness or the simplicity, either way, once again her daughter had left her with nothing to say.

❧

*A*t my feet sat the Toyo. I hadn't used it in twelve years. The magazine had suggested

I take the photos to accompany the article. Celine Arneaux turning seventy-five. Her granddaughter, twenty-five. The Return to the Cabin, as documented by Arneaux herself.

I thought the idea obvious. I also thought they were perhaps humoring an old woman. I agreed. I couldn't stand the thought of someone else's miserable photographs of my cabin, my land, or Cam.

Before photography, portraits on glass or porcelain were fired in the ovens, likenesses preserved forever. The photograph of my mother's father and his two brothers, now on my bureau, was the first thing she unpacked when we moved from Shanghai to Paris. In front of the three seated men, the photographer had arranged potted plum blossom, narcissi and chrysanthemums, emblematic of longevity, good fortune and a life of peace. Behind them hung a scroll with thick black characters: "Future generations, remember to stay united."

When I was a child, my older Chinese relatives said that your soul was absorbed into the machine, and even if that didn't happen, you were sure to become very ill. When that photo of my grandfather and great-uncles had been taken, there'd been a doctor in attendance in case of harm. I told Cam stories like this but she, of course, already understood.

I'd given my camera the most cursory of checkups. I planned to rely on mechanical excuses if necessary. I had dusted the ribs of the bellows with a wet fingertip, experimented with the rise and fall of the front standard. Who knew what I could expect of it after twelve years, but going on with the examination felt like trying to raise the dead. Afterwards I could taste on my finger the rubber and dust of the bellows.

The first communication I received from the child, about five months ago, was a postcard of the Statue of Liberty, on which she had written: *Dear Celine: Hello. My name is Alice. Did you have a garden in China? Can you help bring my mother to me?* I had written back: *In the garden of the Shanghai house, my mother planted lilacs. Acacia trees for shade. Metasequoia trees with tiny green buds. Forsythia, dahlias and pots of lilies and ferns in clusters along the wall. The day we left for Paris, she circled the garden, wiping leaves and even rocks with a damp cloth.*

Before that sad day, you could find her, and sometimes my father with her, sitting in wicker chairs arranged on the grass by quiet servants. I remember cushions. Coils of mosquito incense. Chrysanthemum tea in covered cups. Sparrows, and sometimes the sound of the cuckoo. Violin music coming out one of the open windows from the record player.

I could see my mother placing a careful needle on the spinning disc.

I shook my head and concentrated on the slow crawl of airplanes and baggage trucks outside.

What was infuriating was the banality of old age. What was occurring to me had occurred to thousands of seventy-five-year-olds before me.

If memories like these appeared now, unprovoked, what would happen at the cabin?

Movement next to me. The young man sitting to my right had turned to lean towards me.

"Excuse me," he said in English. "Celine Arneaux, right?" He offered a hand. "Steven Liu."

I stared at his hand.

"From *Aperture*." He took back his hand.

My stomach dipped. I concentrated on communicating composure. How long had he been sitting there?

"I know, I know," he went on. "You didn't want me tagging along." He put his hands up, as if surrendering. "That's cool. Don't worry; I'm not like, you know, lurking and stalking."

He said it like it was a song, "Lurking and Stalking." "How reassuring," I said.

He laughed and winked at me. Winked!

"Here's the thing," he said, getting serious. "I just have one or two questions. Small things really. Just some gaps, you know—"

I stared.

He went on. "Just a couple of questions about your mother."

I stood up. "Excuse me," I said. "As I made clear on the phone, I prefer to travel alone." I put my handbag over my arm and walked away before he could answer.

I made my way to the ladies' room carefully, resisting the temptation to feel my way along the corridor walls. I closed a stall door and concentrated on returning my breathing to normal.

My mother? What possible reason could he have for wanting information about her? What if he were there when I came out?

I hadn't slept last night. I never slept well before a trip, and ghosts required more space and time than dreams. What had I been thinking, agreeing to this article? It was taunting the dragon at the mouth of the cave.

Three Cam photos hung beside my bedroom window: the first from each book. The treasure in the cave beyond the dragon: the possibility of recapturing it was apparently too seductive to resist.

I stood up straighter, and looked at the back of the stall door. This is ridiculous, I thought. I do not behave this way.

I walked out of the ladies' room, keeping myself from glancing around.

The child's age hadn't escaped my notice. Six. Cam's age for the second book. Stupid. It meant nothing.

The child had never responded to my description of my mother's garden. Again, my mother.

My seat in the waiting area was empty. So was his. He had moved across the room to a bank of pay phones. He was talking to someone. I sat back down and rechecked my ticket. He was off the phone now. He looked in my direction, but stayed across the room.

I squeezed my eyes shut, then opened them again. Think about something else, I told myself.

My mother showed me how to look at

things. In Shanghai and later in Paris, I cherished outings with her to the markets, but mostly to the public parks, staying out late in the afternoons to hear her list the names of flowers and watch her point at them with her heavy umbrella of tung-oil-painted canvas. Pomegranates, roses, oleanders, midget willows. Pay attention, she would say from her perch on the cool stone bench, her tiny feet barely reaching the gravel path: paying attention to the familiar is as valuable as discovering something new.

In Paris in the late 1920s, her appearance and language attracted the glances of passersby. In the thirties, looking so foreign was even more of an issue. People consistently mistook her for Indochinese or Japanese. My desire to hear what she knew gave way to a desire for her invisibility and silence. After the city was liberated, my father wrote to me: *Mother had to stay inside, as the crowds were throwing anyone who looked Japanese out of windows and off of roofs.*

A twinge. I held the back of my neck. What could he know about my mother? I was tired. I wouldn't sleep on the plane. Perhaps a walk would help. Would he follow? And the thought of young women in the airport cafés, sipping coffee, touching their tablemates, made my limbs heavy. Would every instance of intimacy always fatigue me?

He was on the phone again, a notebook open in front of him. He was taking a lot of notes. He glanced over at me every so often.

The Virginia air now in July would be slow

and wet. Lingering and sticky like fine damp sand. Even the trees perspiring. What would be in bloom? Flowers I'd forgotten. What had happened to the wisteria? I closed my eyes, attempting a tour. The uneven stone wall of my studio. On their lattice frames, rambler roses: red, yellow and white. Below, irises and Sweet William.

In 1966, the summer Cam turned one, we discovered when we arrived from the city that the ivy vines had found their way through the upstairs windows and across the nursery's sloped ceiling. I used it for the first photo in *One*. Cam in her crib, that thin vine making its way across the ceiling behind her.

Even the Communist Chinese were admirers of my early work, the landscapes. After Cam, they weren't as pleased, but they remained respectful. I was a strong and consistent supporter. The Cam photos held more for the Americans. My job was not to please everyone.

This girl, Alice, was full Chinese.

In a week, I'd be seventy-five. My mother had died at seventy-two. I mouthed her name—Huying. One of its meanings: to echo each other from afar.

He was off the phone and making his way towards me.

I closed my eyes and willed images of Cam. Cameron, I said. Cameron. Again and again, like a blanket over a fire.

———

THE LAST PICTURE

A TWELVE-YEAR-OLD in heavy makeup wears a traditional Chinese silk dress. It is several sizes too large. She holds the excess fabric bunched at her hip.

Beneath the dress, she is naked.

She is barefoot and stands as if in fourth position. She is out of focus, attenuated by the heat waves of the bonfire beside her, taller than she is.

In the foreground, the focus is on some determined mongrel flowers.

⟳

*S*umin stole glances at Alice while the girl slept. She was flushed, her bangs sticking to her forehead. Sumin had forgotten how much heat small children generated. She remembered checking on Cam in her crib, alarmed at the baby's temperature even though she knew there was nothing to be alarmed about.

Cam glanced over at her. "Nice hat," she said.

It was a tennis hat with five or six caterpillars embroidered around the rim. Sumin reached up to touch it. "What's wrong with this hat?" she asked.

Cam turned up the air-conditioning. "Worms?" she said.

Sumin still had her hand on her hat like she was worried about wind. "Caterpillars," she said.

Alice clacked her teeth together. Cam didn't

33

comment on it. Sumin assumed it was another "thing."

"You know," she said, "if you hadn't been in such a rush to get back on the road, we wouldn't have left her."

"Mother," Cam said. "You let her go to the bathroom in some gas station by herself." She shook her head. "It's so typical, it's barely worth commenting on."

"What's that supposed to mean?" Sumin said, despite her embarrassment at their elementary-school dynamics.

From the backseat, Alice said, "I don't want to go to Virginia."

Cam said, "It'll be great. I told you. It's where I went as a little girl. There's a pond, and horses, and cows, and a big forest, and—"

Alice said, "I know. I heard you before. I still don't want to go."

Cam looked at her mother.

Sumin turned to Alice. "I know," she said. "I don't want to go either. But it's just something we both gotta do."

"Thanks, Sumin," Cam said. "That's a big help."

"And I don't like Celine," Alice added.

Sumin laughed.

"You're the one who wanted to write to her," Cam said.

Alice didn't answer.

"You'll like her when you meet her," Cam said.

Sumin snorted.

Cam ran her hand through her hair. It was

a new cut. It made her look like an Asian Louise Brooks. Sumin liked it.

"Why are you here anyway?" Cam asked. "It's not like you needed to be."

Sumin couldn't stand this anymore. Over Cam's protests, she insisted they pull off at a depressing highway restaurant in Maryland. Alice said she didn't care what they did.

Inside the restaurant, they hovered by the door. A waitress made no move to greet them. There was an S-shaped counter on one end and circular booths on the other. In between, a metal salad bar looked like it had been wiped with a wet, dirty cloth.

"Oh, yeah," Cam said. "I want to eat here."

They took a booth by the window. Alice immediately went up on her knees, her face to the glass as if even the parking lot would be better than this.

Sumin took in the counter area. "A lot of truckers," she said.

Cam said, "I'm sticking to something on my chair." She held up her plastic-covered menu. There was dried food on it. Alice perked up momentarily, then went back to the window.

Sumin pretended none of this bothered her, and when the waitress came over, she ordered more than she wanted.

Cam ordered french fries and watched the waitress walk away. There were miniature jukeboxes on the tables. As a distraction, Sumin fed a quarter into theirs and punched up two songs. The first began, faintly.

"Oh, God, Sumin," Cam said. "Michael Bolton?"

"He's good," Sumin said, getting warm again.

"Yeah," Cam said, turning back to the menu. "Like you know."

Sumin pulled a WetNap from a Baggie in her purse and gave her face, neck and hands a thorough wipe-down. She tapped Alice on the shoulder and handed her a small tape measure on a key chain. "Here," she said. "Measure some things." Alice went to work.

Cam watched truckers at the counter until the waitress brought their coffees. Sumin poured some of hers into her saucer and then added six half-and-halfs to what remained. Cam watched and then returned her attention to the counter. Alice insisted that she needed to do the same thing. Cam tried to talk her out of it, then ordered another coffee.

Watching Alice repeat her coffee ritual touched Sumin.

Alice asked for a WetNap.

Sumin gave her the whole bag.

Alice wiped her face, her neck, her hands.

Sumin couldn't remember the last time someone had imitated her. "I like reading biographies of dead people," she said to Cam.

Cam looked at her.

Alice sipped her concoction and announced she wanted some milk. With a straw, she told the waitress.

Sumin went on. "Everyone seems equal. Like the slate's been wiped clean, and we're all starting over."

Cam looked back at the counter. Then she said, "Do you try to be like this, or does it come naturally?"

Their food came. Sumin's sandwich was better than she'd expected, and Alice was eating her cheeseburger, and her second song was playing. She gave conversation with her daughter another try.

"I'm thinking," she started, and then paused to give Cam time to focus on her. "I'm thinking of asking Celine for something."

Cam stopped cutting Alice's meat. "Wait," she said. "We can't all be asking her for things."

"That's very generous," Sumin said, and went on anyway. "I'm thinking about asking if she'd be interested in doing a kind of..." She faltered and realized this was the first time she'd tried to put it into words. She looked away. "A kind of an interview. An intimate interview."

"Isn't Grady already doing that?" Cam asked.

"What's 'intimate'?" Alice asked.

Cam blew on a french fry. Her interest was dwindling back to expected levels. "It's when two people are so close that they'll do anything for each other."

Alice seemed to be thinking.

It wasn't the way Sumin would've defined the word. But she hurried on, worried that she'd already lost Cam's interest. "I guess I imagined something more intimate. You know, where she and I would do a Truffaut/Hitchcock kind of thing."

Cam nodded, and sopped a huge amount of

ketchup onto a fry. She drank about half of her water. She tapped Alice's plate with her fork, reminding the girl to eat. She ate another fry.

"Is that so impossible?" Sumin finally said.

Alice said she had to go to the bathroom.

Cam looked at Sumin.

Alice picked up on it. "I can go alone," she said. "Just tell me where it is."

Cam said, "I'll go with you."

Sumin watched them walk across the restaurant. The sight of Cam leading Alice by the hand gave her a pit in her stomach. Inexplicable, but enough to make her even more determined. She took off her hat and folded it into her bag.

"Why is that so outlandish?" she asked when they got back.

Cam got Alice resettled. "Eat your food," she said. She turned to her mother. "Where's the hat?"

"Well?" Sumin said.

"For starters," Cam said, "who are you gonna be—Truffaut or Hitchcock?"

Who *raised* such a daughter? she thought, while Cam finished her french fries, and Sumin got ready, as always, to pick up the check. Who taught her such contempt for me? And the answer came back immediately: I did.

❧

Steven Liu was back. He sat down next to me. How about just one question? A quick one, he promised. It really would help him out.

I told him it was not my job to make his life easier. I put my hand on his arm. "And now," I said. "You must leave me alone."

He took a breath, shook his head slightly, then said I was right; he was sorry. He hoped I'd have a good trip. This time he didn't stay in the waiting area, and I watched him walk down the corridor back towards the terminal.

Shanghai, March 21, 1927. No school in the afternoon because of "the trouble." The General Labor Union, under Communist Party direction, instigated a general strike and an armed insurrection against the warlords and in support of Chiang Kai-shek's approaching Guomindang forces. Six hundred thousand workers participated. Our power went out. Our phones didn't work. Don't worry, my father told my mother and me, they are under strict orders not to harm foreigners. And they didn't. My father considered this noble and fair, and completely reliable.

Chiang himself showed up in Shanghai at the end of March. He issued placating statements to the foreign community. See, my father said. My mother said nothing, more familiar than my father with the ways of Chinese politicians. My father was asked to join the newly formed Society for Common Progress. They met at the house of the chief of detectives of the French Concession, a man whom my father had ministered to. My father went to a few meetings. The Society was supposed to be working for harmony, for some kind of balance between all these forces. In fact, my father told us, it was made up of wealthy Shanghai industrialists, Guomindang leaders, including Chiang, and notorious underworld figures. I announced that I wasn't surprised; the daughter of the chief of detectives was in my class, and I had found her small-minded and arrogant.

My father stopped going to meetings. His reassurances to us about Chiang, about the foreigner's position in Shanghai, came less frequently. But, still, Chiang's massacre shocked everyone. At four a.m. on April 12, the Society for Common Progress attacked all the headquarters of the city's large unions. They came heavily armed, dressed in civilian clothing. Blue cloth with white armbands. Many union members were killed. The knowledge and assistance of the foreign-concession authorities particularly shamed my father. When Shanghai townspeople, workers and students staged a protest the next day, Chiang's troops fired on them, killing nearly a hundred.

"How can we stay?" he said to my mother. I'd sipped my tea, which burned my tongue, and watched them both.

That same month, on the gates to my father's hospital, a sign was posted: *"Refuse Western medicines. They are made with the organs of small children."*

I was looking forward to my twelfth birthday and some people were beginning to suggest the troubles were gone. At street gatherings where this sort of speculation went on, my father said little. Then he told us that we were going back to Paris.

My mother had said that it was going back for *him*. For us, she said, putting an arm around me, it was just going.

Boarding was announced. I stood immediately. Thank God, I thought. I glanced down the corridor, around the waiting room.

The American family I'd tried to avoid was having a disagreement. Nearby neutrals were becoming involved. One of the boys was crying. The father was holding him by the upper arm and shaking him ineffectually. He was bringing his face close, attempting to create authority through proximity. The mother made halfhearted stabs at calming the other boys.

Cam had nothing near the kind of discipline it took to raise a child, but the thought of a small girl clambering around her did hold my interest. Of course, there was no guarantee that she'd be anything like Cam had been. *She knows me*, Cam kept saying about her. *She knows me*. I hadn't known what to make of the comment, but something about it disturbed me. Perhaps the willingness to reveal her need, so unlike her, and so unlike the traits I'd tried to instill.

The old rule for children: *ting-hua*—"heeding the words."

I waited to board, and reassured myself that this family wouldn't be traveling First Class.

Forget about Steven Liu, I said to myself. Out the windows overlooking the runways, the sun. I closed my eyes and felt it.

My father had prepared me for the Paris house. It was his family's house, large and formidable in elegant grey stone with wrought-iron fences and gates. The house of a family whose members cannot remember a time of lack. It was filled with overstuffed furniture, tapestries, a meticulously labeled collection of art, Chinese porcelain and bronzes.

He had not prepared me for the family living in that house. When we first arrived, his family moved down the front steps as one to greet us, and I took a step back. My mother nudged me. Two toddlers later to be introduced as cousins saw her and began crying. One of my father's sisters said to her: "Excuse the babies. They are not used to foreigners."

I felt lucky that they didn't mean me. Later that night, I overheard my grandmother talking to my father.

"You must not," she was saying, "have any more children."

He was quiet.

Her voice came again. There was no place for them in this world. She paused. He knew this.

It wasn't just anger I felt rising through me. It was anger and determination. This pale angular woman and my father, who refused to protest: I would make them both crumble under the iron evidence that I was someone who could belong anywhere.

During the war, my father had taken Picasso as his model for behavior under the Occupation. Leaving Paris was never an option.

There, he seemed impervious to the tidal shifts of war and politics. He never pretended to approve of the Nazis or Pétain. As before, his work came first. This dignity in the face of something as formidable as the Nazis made his cowardice in the face of his mother even harder to bear. After the war, I considered that cowardice even more of a betrayal.

I was next in line. He was back, touching my elbow.

"Have a good trip," he said. "I'm sorry." He stepped away and watched me board.

The stewardess had to ask for my ticket twice, and I wouldn't look back and I wouldn't hurry myself down the airway.

That last week in China, my mother took me a final time to the hill where the ancestors were buried. To look at the views. The servants brought lacquer boxes filled with lunch. My mother spent hours dusting the engraved characters of each headstone's poem. I, as always, stood off to the side, looking down the mountain.

Without meaning to, my father taught me how different I looked from his family by showing me photographs before we left for Paris. Once we got there, my mother taught me by example how I could use that difference.

For the wealthy, hairdressers, seamstresses, manicurists, even perfumers would make house calls. My mother refused appointments with all of them. She wouldn't go to the perfume shop of Richard Hudnut on Rue de la Paix, though it was where everyone of her class went. She made her own perfume by soaking a mixture of flowers in her wash-basin overnight. She was suspicious of the French colognes. She never gave up her Chinese dress or hairstyles. She took particular care of her hair. She wore flowers at the base of her bun, and shampooed and rinsed in two complete cycles. She used her wooden combs from her childhood, soaking them in the juice of pomelo seeds.

Her hair made my father's female relatives forget, momentarily, my mother's horrible feet. When I saw the way they looked at her hair, I understood that difference could be manipulated to produce envy.

❧

The plane was taking off. A surge. A sinking stomach. But still, relief at leaving Steven Liu far below. I closed my eyes.

I did Cam's hair the way my mother had done mine: a flowering ponytail at the top of my head. We called it "coconut palm." I would do Alice's hair the same way. I opened my eyes. I realized I didn't even know what Alice's hair looked like. I folded my hands in my lap. Ridiculous. I would have nothing to do with Alice.

It was necessary to stop thinking of my mother. On a plate I knew exactly how to ease a body into darkness. Why was this so different? What was the technique?

An older woman across from me was also

traveling alone, her profile striking against the window glare. She looked over. Her face had the untroubled look that the upper-class French are such geniuses at maintaining. I could just imagine her in prewar Paris, refusing to see the misfortune around her. She had done her best to ignore the Depression in the first half of the decade, why should she pay attention to foreign affairs now? My father, on the other hand, had already begun looking into my passage to the States. The tidal shifts of politics mattered more, apparently, to one's daughter than to oneself. I thought about telling this woman about Steven Liu. Despite myself, I smiled at her. She nodded.

I was never bored when alone; I grew easily bored with others. So I lived within my own four walls. A few people were all I needed. I could stand only a few at a time anyway. It didn't mean I didn't ache. But I had to live according to my own will, or why bother?

This was part of the draw of photographs, the gauging of the physical extent of losses, the size of longing or regret. Cameron was above all a companion, where before there'd been no one. This was what she had said about the girl: I'm not alone anymore.

I refused the breakfast service—tiny portions of food served with an airline's attempts at style. I tried to read. Colette on Southern France. Durás and the foods her Chinese lover discovered for her: moon cakes, white with pink markings. Crushed lichee sprinkled with sesame seeds. Bean with rose petals. Ginger

45

with quince. My painter and I had tried eating only American food: corned-beef hash, apple pie with cheese, something called Philly Cheese Steaks. We had failed, our tongues too disgusted to go on, and we had ended up gorging ourselves on dinner at a Chinese restaurant that we never went back to.

Risk was what I'd wanted. Risk was what Cam had brought, and had maintained, at least until she turned twelve.

I'd named her. In our family, grandmothers named the children; no one knew how or why the usual tradition had been altered. My grandmothers had named me: Celine from my father's mother, Li Na from my mother's. My mother named Sumin. When it was my turn, I named Sumin's baby after Julia Margaret Cameron, a woman who knew how to dissolve a body into the recesses of shadow. She seemed to have intimidated her subjects into cooperation. Carlyle had said about his portrait, "It is as if it suddenly began to speak, terrifically ugly and woe-begone."

Sumin wondered if the camera/Cameron connections were too obvious. The comment had been unworthy of a response.

How much of all this could Steven Liu, could Grady, know?

Cam changed the landscape of that place. The main elements had always been sleep, water, darkness and light. She added the naked body.

———

UNTITLED

A NEGLECTED CEMETERY in the middle of thick woods. The white headstones tip and fall in all directions against the blackness of the tree trunks around them.

In the left background, the largest of the trees. A girl perched on the roots, her head back against the trunk. It has rained recently. Everything is wet. The girl's hair sticks to her face.

Her eyes are closed. Her mouth open slightly. She is touching herself. It's impossible to tell where her fingers end and the vee of her legs begins.

⌐

$\mathcal{A}$lice didn't want to get back in the car. Cam tried a variety of things that had no effect.

Sumin said, "We're leaving. You're welcome to stay here." She climbed into the passenger seat and closed the door. "Start the car, Cam."

Cam was enough at a loss to do as her mother said. Sumin told her to pull out of the parking space. Alice let out a high-pitched scream. Cam stopped the car, and Sumin leaned forward to let Alice into the backseat.

Nobody said anything as they made their way back to the highway.

Then Cam said, "Abandonment tricks are

probably not the best idea in her case." She turned and apologized to Alice.

Sumin stared at the road. She had never heard Cam apologize to anyone. She said, "She's in the car, isn't she?"

Alice said, "Yes, but you forget how stupid you are."

Sumin was surprised at how hurtful the comment was. She turned to Cam. "Good luck convincing Celine of this idyllic relationship," she said.

Cam looked genuinely pained, and Sumin felt bad. "Well, if anyone can do it, you can," she offered.

They accelerated to pass a station wagon. The kids in the back waved at Alice. She ignored them.

"When's the last time you looked at the books?" Cam asked her mother.

The night before in fact, home with Grady, enduring more poring over the photos, more of his questions. For the last three months, he'd been trying to get her interested in his research on her mother. He was stunned by how little she knew and appalled by how little she wanted to know. He asked her questions, but she wasn't supposed to look at his notes. He wanted her contribution to this article to be as "normal" as possible. He explained in his I'll-go-slow-so-you-can-follow voice that the interviewer normally doesn't live with the subject's daughter.

His preparations had been like Celine's before her first photo session with Cam:

choices that left Sumin with the consequences.

She had made dinner. He liked when she prepared Chinese food. It made them both feel good to have her act Chinese. On their second date he'd said that he didn't mean to pry, but she looked much more Asian than her mother. She'd been pleased, and had explained. Fascinating, he had finally said, and for part of the dinner she'd decided to believe he meant her.

They had met in a journalism class Grady had taught at the New School. He had seemed so sure of himself and his talents. So grown-up. And something else. Sumin had described it to Cam this way: he seemed so comfortable in the world and he seemed to take for granted that other people would feel the same way. Cam had suggested that Sumin was probably hoping some of that would rub off on her. Yes, Sumin had agreed, like playing tennis with someone who's better than you are.

Sumin had summoned up her courage and made an appointment to talk with him about her final project, something to do with her mother, and he had been beside himself with delight to discover who her mother was. Office hours stretched into coffee; coffee stretched into dinner and Sumin talked and talked, using her mother as currency with this tall, grey-haired man.

Now, in the car, a gesture he'd made last night continued to bother her. He'd been whining about how little he knew about Celine's family. Sumin had, by that point, been finding it difficult to drum up sympathy for his position.

From the kitchen sink, she'd said, "*I'm* her family." She returned to the dining table. Grady was finishing off his meal with a pile of assorted nuts. Some of the shells were as far as five or six feet from the table.

She stood beside him and picked up shell pieces from around his napkin. He wiped his hands off over her hands, the lord making the servant's work easier. "You know what I mean. Her father, her mother. That kind of family."

She recited: "He was a French doctor in Shanghai. She was the only daughter of a wealthy merchant family. They moved to Paris when Celine was twelve. Celine moved to the States in 'thirty-nine. The father died in 'fifty-six. The mother moved back to China in 1962. *She* died a few years after that."

This was when he'd made the gesture. Like she'd touched on something crucial. A lift of the finger, as if a puppeteer had accidentally pulled a string. "Do you know what she died of?" he asked.

She'd been annoyed with their whole conversation. She'd tried to put an end to it. "She was old. She died."

Cam tapped her on the forehead. "Hello?" she said.

Sumin stared at her.

Alice said, "She's not listening to you." It was unclear whom she was referring to.

"Do you know anything about Huying?" Sumin asked her daughter.

"Who's Huying?" Cam said, and her mother lapsed into silence again.

She and Grady had been over what she knew, years ago. She had met her grandmother only once, in 1956 for her grandfather's funeral. Celine herself had only gone back to Paris twice in the years between the end of the war and her father's death, and both times she had left Sumin with a friend, despite Sumin's desperate negotiations to be taken. Sumin had never had the courage to ask, then or later, why Celine had gone home so rarely.

What Sumin remembered most about the funeral was Huying's poise in the face of her grief. Sumin had commented on that to Celine on their way back to the States, and Celine had told her not to react like a Westerner. Perhaps Huying had loved her husband too much to display her grief.

Sumin had been so surprised by her mother's vehemence that she hadn't pursued the subject.

The three women hadn't been at the cabin together for twelve years, since *Twelve*. A nice symmetry. They'd never been there with anyone else for any extended period of time. *Nu Ren Guo* was what Celine had called it: an Empire of Women. *Celine Guo* was what Cam called it.

It seemed dangerous to bring Grady there, and she didn't know why. Her anxiety annoyed her, but remained convincing.

Last night, he'd tried to be nice. He'd asked if she was looking forward to seeing her mother. He'd asked if she thought it would be

51

fun to have a little kid around the cabin again. She'd shot him a look, but there hadn't seemed to have been anything behind the question. A few years ago, he had suggested adopting. He'd pointed out that she knew what it was like to raise a child; he didn't. He typed her a little note and framed it in a small purple frame: *I want you to be a mother again.* It would give them, he argued, a way to literally embody that third thing that was created by the two of them. It was a beautiful sentiment and still she said she was too old; it was too much work; she loved their life the way it was. She listed genuine reasons and still felt she was being dishonest. Finally, he told her the only reason she didn't want to be a mother again was that it wouldn't leave her enough time to obsess about being a daughter. It was a moment of perception that she still hadn't completely forgiven him for.

In the years since Celine had moved back to Paris, Sumin had seen her mother a handful of times. Celine had been on junkets to lecture, or present awards to young photographers, or—twice—to oversee the donation of letters and prints to The Asia Society. Sumin had met her for lunch or tea. None of the visits had gone well. Celine had been utterly uncurious about her daughter's life. Occasionally she'd taken time out for an insult. Sumin had kept her poise completely until returning home.

She should've welcomed the lack of interest. If you looked at it a certain way, it took some of the pressure off.

When they were first living together, Grady had been a big help. He would insist that Celine loved her. He would come up with all sorts of theories for her mutated way of showing it.

"I love you," he'd said last night, tucking her in for what would be a completely sleepless night. It had been a good thing for him to do.

Even so, there she was, fixed on her mother. People came and went, offering various things, and there she always was, fixed on her mother.

A few months ago, right around when Cam got Alice, Sumin had told Grady that she didn't think it—they—were working out. She'd wanted to know why he wanted to be with her. What could he possibly get from being with her? That conversation had gone nowhere and he'd ended up hugging her and suggesting they just give it some time. Since then they'd lived in a kind of limbo state, treading delicately around each other like houseguests.

So last night, when he'd told her he loved her, she'd squeezed his forearm and said, "I know you do." He did his I'm Sad for You walk away from the bed. She felt bad for hurting him. We're all hurting, she thought, and then was angry with herself for thinking just the kind of thing her mother expected from her.

⁓

*S*olitude. Some days a cool hand on my forehead, other days just manageable, and others as if I were suffocating in a windowless cell.

Was he making more phone calls? I waved my hand impatiently. Who cared what young Steven Liu was doing?

The cabin used to provide sleep. The darkness in the bedrooms upstairs, with their sloped roofs and windows that reached to the floor. Lying there, I could see the outline of my camera and tripod sentinel-like in the corner. I would tuck the sheet beneath my arms and imagine myself the only living being in the night.

Before Sumin, I used to walk with the camera in New York. A big one was like carrying a baby who hadn't learned to lock her legs around your waist. But baby and camera were impossible to manage at once. The tripod and the camera bumped and knocked, and everything seemed to be made of corners. Sumin remained made of corners. But the box became an extension of my hands, and the three-legged stand fit the curve of my arm.

No one was more surprised than I at my desire to have the baby. I've never discovered a satisfactory answer to the question of where that desire sprang from, or why it did not translate to unadulterated love for the child. But first and foremost, I was *un imagier*. Maternity found time when it had to.

Of course it had to do with making things mine. But I never took Cam from her mother in the banal sense. And for Sumin, Cam was a way to stay connected to me. It was a gift.

Last night, I walked and walked. Past the houses where my father used to take me, and sometimes, until sentiment towards foreigners became too volatile, my mother to the fancy dress balls of the thirties. I remembered a dance floor resting on tiny springs, so you felt truly as if floating on air.

I stared into the lit windows of ground-floor apartments. I saw curio cabinets and living-room paintings. Dubious lace drapes and mystifying wooden shutters. In one house, a laughing host, holding a wineglass carelessly. I found myself hoping he had a maroon rug beneath. In another, a lovely Irish-haired woman, slim, in a Japanese kimono, moving from one exposed room to another. I followed at her pace, our steps mirroring each other's.

So when people insisted that I'd used Cam, I said: with imaginative intent. Sumin's uses were quite different. And Cam? She thinks that she and Alice are meant for each other, that they were born to help each other. But when she speaks of her, it's in terms of what the girl can do for her. There's no escaping the self-ishness of motherhood.

❧

Maryland seemed to be going on too long.

"I've been looking at the books over and over," Cam said. She was driving with one hand. "You know. For the portrait."

Cam painted portraits; they were like collages. People's faces were always orange or green. She painted the way Celine took pictures: as if squeezing the life out of her subjects. Celine thought her job was to reveal the flaws. Cam had a related way of making everyone look uglier than necessary.

She'd started out by painting Celine over and over again. As an undergraduate, she'd showed Sumin some of her early work. Sumin had asked whether she was really going to be this psychologically uncomplicated, and that had been the end of sharing.

"That was an uncharacteristic comment of yours, the other day," Cam had remarked a week or so later. "Not only uncharacteristically mean, but uncharacteristically astute." And they had left it at that.

Now, Sumin's official position was that she didn't know what to make of Cam's portraits. She had done one for her grandmother's birthday, but wouldn't say what it was of. It was wrapped in brown paper, sharing space with Alice in the backseat. Sumin had wondered for years how Cam would paint her. She could just imagine, she thought dismally.

She asked Alice if she'd seen the portrait. Alice shook her head. "She doesn't show me anything," she said.

"Me neither," Sumin said.

Cam ignored them. "You know what it's like, to look at images and see that the world is familiar, but I'm not? It's like looking at somebody else's pictures."

A small, slow wave went through Sumin. She tucked her hands between her thighs and the vinyl seat covers. "Pictures of somebody else may not be so bad," she said.

Alice leaned forward, suddenly interested. She said to Sumin, "Why aren't there any pictures of you?"

Cam glanced at her mother. Sumin's small wave broke, the sadness running quietly in all directions.

Cam filled the silence. "There are," she said. "There's that one, that one that was taken when you were little." She nodded at her mother. She looked at Alice in the rearview mirror. "It was published in a book called *Children of the World*."

It had actually been taken by a hapless suitor of Celine's. Sumin was two or three years old, dressed in silk pajamas. She was holding a tulip, half-hidden by the door to Celine's sitting room in their New York apartment. There were hints of opulence behind her: the round arm of a damask sofa; the ornately carved door, a fairy-tale key resting in its lock.

Alice didn't ask for details. "But why only one?" she asked. "Where was your mom?"

The sun ricocheted off the chrome of the side mirrors. Again, Cam stepped in, making excuses. Maybe Alice's presence was having some kind of nice-person effect on her. Whatever the reason, this new version of her was disquieting.

"*I'll* explain," Sumin said. And she told

about the one and only time her mother had taken photos of her. Cam had never asked about it. No one had. Sumin told it slowly and carefully, the way you carry a pitcher filled to the brim with something that will stain, or talk to a child when you want her to understand you the first time.

It was autumn of 1966, at the cabin during the shooting of *One*. Cam had been too crabby to deal with, and Celine had appeared in Sumin's doorway and had handed her old clothes, bamboo fans, and big sheets of white paper with black calligraphy scrawled across them. Come on, come on, she had said, and Sumin had gathered everything together, trying not to crush the paper, and had followed.

The photos had been taken in the studio over the course of two days. In Celine's judgment, they weren't very good. They were tableaux designed to comment on the tumult in China at the time. As Grady had explained it to her over and over, in February of that year, Jiang Qing, Mao's wife, and cultural workers for the People's Liberation Army had met and concluded that the Chinese cultural garden was overgrown with "anti-socialist poisonous weeds." This forum would be the beginning of the Great Proletariat Cultural Revolution. Mao's edicts against the "four old" elements within Chinese society—old customs, old habits, old culture and old thinking—were carried out by the Red Guards, squads of students declared to be the vanguard of the new revolution, in increasingly violent ways. According to Grady, the fall of 1966 was the worst time. Schools were closed, buildings were demolished, teachers, friends and parents were attacked. Red Guards began to turn on anyone or anything that held them in check.

When her friends asked about the situation, Celine said that all of it brought back her father's descriptions of denunciations in occupied Paris, but she wouldn't answer any of Sumin's queries. Sumin hadn't known what to think herself. She chose not to think too much about it. She chose to be as happy as she could, safe in Virginia with her new daughter, and now, with some welcome attention from her mother.

In the studio for those two days of shooting, Sumin spent her time with her arms spread, her body bent at the waist, a dunce cap decorated with the characters *niugui sheshen*: cow ghosts and snake spirits. Or squeezed into an old turquoise *qipao*, too small to be one of Celine's, with red satin sandals hung around her neck. For a few of the setups, she carried a sign: *Huacheng meinu de she*: snake in the disguise of a beautiful woman. For all of them, Celine had made her up to look much older, her hair in the traditional bun circled in white thread to indicate the status of widow.

Throughout, Celine had been preoccupied and angry. She'd been even less tolerant of questions than usual. When Sumin had asked whose *qipao* this was, Celine had left the room. She'd returned twenty minutes later. In the meantime, Sumin had sat cross-legged on the floor and had picked at and unraveled the intricate stitching on the hems.

Nothing had come of the photos. Celine made a few prints, and then told Sumin that she'd destroyed the negatives. Sumin didn't tell Cam and Alice that she'd managed to save some of the prints in the bottom of a file box under bank statements and bundles of Christmas cards. She didn't share her reasons for saving them. They were an embarrassment to her: Did she need proof of a connection so much that she nostalgically transformed memories such as that?

When Cam was in high school, Sumin had left one of the prints on her desk with a note: *Thought you might like this*. Cam had not responded—Sumin hadn't even been sure if Cam realized the woman in the photo was her mother—and Sumin hadn't pursued it. And now, in the car, Cam didn't seem to see the connection. She was acting as she always acted. For years, her facial expression when listening to her mother had been: Tell Me Something I Don't Know.

Sumin hadn't shown them to anyone else; instead, she'd continued to trot out what she'd always said when people asked if her mother had taken photos of her, something she'd read somewhere: It was like the shoe-maker's daughter going barefoot.

Both Alice and Cam were quiet. A truck passed them and the car shook.

Alice said, "Why isn't Grady driving with us anyway?" She'd met Grady only a couple of times, but she liked him; that was clear to everyone. It bothered Sumin more than she liked to admit.

"He'll be there tomorrow," Cam said.

"You mean after this night?" Alice asked.

"Yes," Cam said.

"You mean one night and then it's tomorrow?" Alice asked.

Cam was losing patience. "As I said, yes; one night."

"You're mad a lot," Alice said quietly.

Anger was Cam's central emotion. Sumin had always believed it gave her daughter power. Alice had said the word like it was a flaw.

Cam said, "I don't mean to be mad." Then she added, "He's waiting for something he needs for the article."

This seemed to satisfy Alice; at least, she fell into silence. Sumin concentrated on the after-effects of telling the story of the photos, and wondered mildly how Cam had known why Grady was staying in the city an extra night.

Then Alice said, "But there are still a lot more photos of Cam, right?"

"Right," Cam finally said, and Sumin's head filled with the familiar, overwhelming pressure of being alone in the presence of others.

❧

I gave up on reading. I felt as though I were here involuntarily. I walked the aisles.

Almost to the end of the plane, I was stopped

by a woman's hand on my arm. I looked down. A Chinese woman, close to my age, in a blue cotton pantsuit that marked her as old-fashioned Mainland.

"Excuse me," she said in English, standing up. She was short enough to stand upright without coming out into the aisle.

"I'm sorry," she said, "but you are Li Na?"

I nodded.

She didn't expect me to remember her; we had met only once or twice, after my mother had moved back to China. She was Hsing Chiang, a friend of my mother's housekeeper. She had known my mother a little.

Was this a joke? I thought. A spy movie?

The stewardess came by with the drink cart, and we retreated to the noisy rear of the plane. We switched to Chinese.

She was so sorry about my mother. She was delighted with running into me. It was such a coincidence, as she had just recently been contacted by a reporter, someone doing an article about me.

Had it been Grady or Steven Liu? How had either of them gotten a hold of this woman's name? And why?

I explained about the article. It was curious, I said, that he would have been interested in contacting her. The article had much more to do with my art than with my connections to China.

She nodded.

We squeezed together to make room for someone on his way to the bathrooms.

"What was the reporter's name?" I asked. She couldn't remember.

"What did he ask you about?" I finally said.

She waved a hand. "Oh, many things." She put her hand on my arm for the second time. "I hope I haven't offended you by speaking with him," she said.

The stewardess came back with her cart. We had to rearrange ourselves.

Of course not, I told her. It was good he was being so thorough.

She went on at length about her destination. She was visiting her sister. It was her first trip to the United States. It had taken years of planning, and she had been given only a week's visa, but she was excited.

I listened with one ear. The housekeeper had been from Mother's old life, the daughter of her nanny in Shanghai. Her name was Chou Yuan. She'd made me uncomfortable. Her whole being seemed to say: You. You are not good enough for this woman who is your mother. Why had he ferreted this woman out?

She touched my arm. And, she said smiling widely, she wanted to congratulate me on the newest member of my family. A girl, she had heard.

The back of my neck reacted before my head. He *had* been thorough.

I asked her how well she had known Chou Yuan. They were neighbors. This told me nothing.

Suddenly everyone was coming back to use

the bathrooms. It was impossible to stay where we were. I walked her back to her seat and stood for a minute more. She took up her knitting, continuing about what a coincidence this was.

I stood there a little longer, then, annoyed with myself, told her to have a good trip and headed back to the front of the plane.

I couldn't sit. I went to the door and stared out the small window until the sky swam. There was no horizon. My head was pounding. There was no way of knowing what kind of information this woman had. There was no way of knowing what she'd talked about. My head. I took a breath.

My technique: From the best two negatives, I always made four contact prints. The smoothness of albumen paper. More than a century ago, the paper most commonly used, despite its instability, the ease with which the image could fade. Coated in egg white and a mixture of dissolved potassium bromide and acetic acid. The print was squeezed between a metal plate and a heated cylinder in a burnisher to give it a gloss. The Dresden Albumenizing Co., the largest in the world, used sixty thousand eggs a day. Girls in factories did nothing all day but separate whites from yolks. The yolks were sent off to be used in the preparation of patent leather. Sixty thousand a day! That art began with such quotidian unhappiness still amazed me.

The white stock, clean and direct, presented, unveiled, all that the negative had to give. At times for added gloss on the finished print, I used a coat of wax.

There was an ordinary level of life and an extraordinary level. After twelve, the extraordinary was gone. At the time I had thought that meant the extraordinary in Cam. I didn't understand, at first, what that disappearance would mean for all my work.

Reviewers had called her "an Oriental angel, a miraculous apparition." The one from New Jersey who always claimed New York called her "a willing collaborator." The noun brought back the special venom my father reserved for colleagues who had reaped the benefits of the Occupation.

The plane banked and the sun hit the plastic of the window. I looked up the aisle. I couldn't see Hsing Chiang. Do not think about her, I told myself.

Cam's imperfections—the disappearance of her mysteries—were my limitations, not my responsibilities. If I confirmed her as collaborator, she shared responsibility for my successes and my failures.

❧

They had finally crossed into Virginia. It wasn't too far now. The same station wagon from hours ago passed them. The girl waved again. Alice ignored her again, but as they moved into the exit lane, Sumin noticed Alice sneaking a final peek at the other girl.

It wasn't the most practical place to get

groceries. There were stores closer to the cabin, but it was what they'd always done, and it was the best place around. When the trip had been planned, one of the first things Sumin had checked was whether the market was still there. She remembered sharing her delight with Alice, who had been somewhat understated in her response.

But getting out of the car and into the store raised everyone's spirits.

Nothing had changed. The produce was in wooden crates along one wall, and everyone crouched and dug around in them. The crates were not the fake ones you could buy at places like Pier 1. They had real dirt in them.

And anyway, it had what they wanted: ginger and herbal teas, that kind of stuff. And everything on Celine's list.

Visits from Celine, even if few and far between, required the sort of preparatory work reserved for rock stars or heads of state. Besides the obvious—hotel reservations and arranged meetings—there was the baroque: all the fixtures in her room needed to have bulbs brighter than one hundred watts. And so on.

For the week, Sumin had managed to whittle her responsibilities down to this shopping list and checking the cleaning woman's job at the cabin.

The list looked like something from a scavenger hunt: Asian pears, Brazil nuts in the shell, colored wooden toothpicks, night-light bulbs. Cam drifted along behind her, leaning her forearms on the shopping cart. She was swaying her hips back and forth and singing softly to herself. Alice was cross-legged in the cart, facing front. She absentmindedly snapped her fingers to Cam's humming.

"Sometimes I'm so *black*," Cam said. She did a bump and grind and took her mother by the hands, pulling her into a dance. Alice, and others, stared. Sumin smiled and blushed.

"Here, Aretha," she said, handing Cam the list. "You guys do the Empress's shopping."

"I need to call my mother," Alice said.

Cam lowered her voice and told her that they couldn't do that right now, but they would later, from the cabin. She put her head close to the girl's. "Okay?" she said.

"Okay," Alice said.

Cam took the list from her mother without looking at it and wandered back to the front of the store. She left the cart and Alice. The girl had black, black hair, just like Cam's.

Sumin had handed her two cucumbers and a package of dried figs before Cam sashayed back down the aisle with a bar of Neutrogena soap and a bundle of cattails. Only the cattails had been on the list.

"These were a great idea," she said, shaking them at her mother. She passed them to Alice, who held them in her arms like a baby.

Sumin took the list back and told her daughter to be at the cashier in fifteen minutes.

In the cereal aisle, Alice announced that she had heard Sumin and Cam's conversation about her in the car.

Sumin nodded. "Pretending to sleep. That's a good way to learn things."

Alice rearranged herself and examined the impressions on her legs that the cart had made.

"So," Sumin said. "What do you think of all this?"

Alice shrugged and pointed at some boxes on the lowest shelf. "Fruit Roll-Ups," she said.

They looked at the boxes.

Alice said, "Cam doesn't let me get them."

"Well, we better not get her angry at us," Sumin said and resumed their stroll down the aisle.

Alice said, "Celine is trying to get me back to my mother."

Sumin kept pushing. "I know," she said and waited.

Alice shook her bangs back and forth, a tic she had developed since moving in with Cam. "I miss my mother," she said.

"I'm sure you do," Sumin said, trying to make her voice softer than it usually was.

"Celine is very...very...," Alice faltered.

Sumin didn't say anything.

"Well, she could bring my mother here," Alice said matter-of-factly. She looked up. "Can we get some of those Fruit Roll-Ups?"

Sumin asked if Cam knew how Alice felt.

Alice shrugged again.

Inexplicably, the thought of Cam's vulnerability made Sumin annoyed with Cam. This made her annoyed with herself. This made her more annoyed with Cam.

She wheeled back to the Fruit Roll-Ups aisle, threw three boxes into the cart and penciled them in at the bottom of the list.

⁓

While they checked out, Cam leafed through *Elle*.

"Look at all this stuff," she said, without looking.

Sumin unloaded the groceries around her.

"Marmite? Star fruit?" Cam asked. She took in the Fruit Roll-Ups. "Who are these for?"

Sumin held up the list.

Cam looked at her mother, and then at Alice. "Whatever," she said.

They watched the cashier adding things up. Alice was grinning.

"Why do we do this for her?" Cam asked.

Sumin handed the cashier some money.

"She could've had Jeeves or whoever stop on the way from the airport," Cam said.

Sumin tucked the change into its proper place in her bag, lifted Alice out of the cart to replace her with the bags. As Alice's face passed, the girl brushed her nose back and forth across Sumin's cheek. Sumin loaded the bags and wondered what her cheek had felt like.

Cam was blocking the way. Sumin waited and then wheeled the cart awkwardly around her, and headed for the door. "We do this for the same reason that you didn't say no during shoots."

Even Alice glanced up at the tone of her voice.

The automatic doors clumped shut behind them.

"You could've," Sumin added.

Cam dipped her head and looked at her mother over her sunglasses. "Is something bothering you?"

The station wagon from the highway was parked nearby, like part of a suspense movie. Little feet were pressed against the back window. "She listened to you back then. She still listens to you," Sumin said, though Cam hadn't said otherwise.

They got to the car, and Sumin opened the trunk.

"I don't think so," was all Cam finally said.

That was what she'd said the summer she was ten, when she'd come to Sumin, complaining, and Sumin had told her that she could always say no. Cam had said, "I don't think so," with that same tone. "Don't you know even *that*?" she'd then asked, frustrated. "Don't you know even *that* by now?"

"Let's switch," Sumin said, slamming the trunk shut. "I feel like driving."

*W*ithin a half-hour, they were lost. She blamed it on Cam.

They'd barely gotten out of the parking lot when Cam had said that it was, when you thought about it, pretty flattering to be the one thing that had enticed a great photographer back to her art after a ten-year dry spell.

Alice was in the back, sucking on a strawberry Roll-Up. Her fingers and lips were already stained pink.

"It must be," Sumin said, watching for their turnoff. "If you think about it."

"I mean," Cam said, "even now people are impressed. You can see it." She rolled the window up and down an inch or so. "Of course their next reaction, if they know the photos—and they *always* know the photos—is to look at me like they expected someone else." She lifted her skirt up over the air vents. She was wearing a rayon miniskirt and a tank top without a bra. They were the kind of clothes Sumin wished she could wear.

"Especially the men," Cam added. "I mean, what am I supposed to say?"

Sumin passed a tractor pulling a precarious load of hay. "I wouldn't know," she said. She glanced at Cam's feet. The map was under them.

"I want to ride a tractor," Alice said. She pressed her sticky face against her window, staring back at the farmer.

Cam looked down at the gear shift. "Uh, Sumin? Shift up?"

The engine was whining. Sumin shifted up.

"I wouldn't flatter myself too much about that," she said.

"About knowing when to shift?" Cam asked, propping one foot up on the dash.

"Cam?" Alice said.

"Yes?" Cam said.

Sumin reached over and pushed the foot off, wiping the scuff mark it had left. "About being the one and only thing that got her back to work."

"Why not?" Cam said. "She always says that until me there wasn't anything worth looking at in those years after the landscapes."

"I want to ride a tractor," Alice said.

"Yeah," Sumin said. "Or she'll tell you she was working on other things. Or she'll tell you it was to spend more time with me. What *I'm* telling you is that she didn't have much of a choice."

They'd talked about this before.

"Yeah, yeah," Cam said. "I know. The blacklisting thing."

Starting in 1956, their mail had been monitored. Celine wasn't a Party member, but she'd still been up in front of some part of HUAC. Someone had even talked to fourteen-year-old Sumin. Sumin remembered him as very nice, and a little embarrassed. Money had seemed to be disappearing into various unidentified places. Every now and then Celine would dress up and go somewhere, touching Sumin on the head in an uncommon expression of maternal tenderness before she left. Slowly, over the years, Sumin had pieced together the fact that her mother's enormous popularity in China and her extensive government contacts weren't advantages in the States.

Alice kicked the back of Cam's seat.

Cam turned around. "Alice. Please. What do you want?"

"I want to ride a tractor."

Cam looked around the car. "Do I have a tractor?" she said. "Am I keeping you from a tractor?"

"I bet we'll be able to find one at the cabin for you to ride," Sumin said.

Alice settled back into her seat.

Back then Celine had seemed genuinely worried for the first time Sumin could remember, and the mood lasted for years. She'd later learned that for four years, from 1956 to 1960, the only photos shown or published were shown or published in China or France, under Celine's Chinese name. Which was fine, but not enough. And then even after the blacklist was officially lifted, there were still no photos, though Celine went into her darkroom every day, notifying Sumin that she was not to be disturbed. And then along came Cam.

"She'd needed a subject," Sumin said. Cam looked bored. "To get her the attention, the money, the everything she thought she deserved. A grandmother and granddaughter. How much more American could you get?"

"You seem determined to burst my bubble," Cam said, as though her mother were incapable of that.

"A big one," Alice said.

"Shouldn't you be checking the map?" Sumin said. "We should've gotten to 522 already."

"Did anybody hear me?" Alice said. "A big one."

"Yes," Sumin said. "Of course, a big one." She looked back at Cam.

"We're fine," Cam said. She didn't move.

"Shouldn't you check?"

Alice leaned forward, grabbing the seat with her incredibly sticky fingers. "Are we lost?" she asked hopefully.

Cam rolled her eyes. "No, we are not lost," she said. She made a production of opening the map, refolding it, shaking it in her mother's face. She stabbed a spot near the top. "We're fine. The intersection's in like..." She paused to do the math. "...five miles." She dropped the whole thing back on the floor. "Outside of What's-Its-Name. Don't you remember anything? What is this, the nine-thousandth time you've made this drive?"

"I think we passed White Post a ways back," Sumin said.

"We passed a miniature golf course," Alice said.

Cam said, "No."

"Yes we did," Alice insisted.

"Could you be any more imperious?" Sumin asked.

"If I'm right, I'm right," Cam said.

Fine, Sumin thought. Let's get lost. Where do I have to be?

Alice complained that the portrait and the groceries made it too crowded in the backseat. She asked if she could have another Fruit Roll-Up. A different flavor. Sumin said yes and Cam grumbled that Celine was going to be pretty annoyed that all her Fruit Roll-Ups were gone.

"You'll notice," Sumin ventured, "that the photos didn't start getting—controversial—until the second book. Until it was safe—even beneficial—to get controversial."

Cam just sat there, like her mother hadn't said anything at all, and Sumin watched the road for something familiar. She'd always known that having Cam would affect her relationship with her mother. She just hadn't known how.

She remembered going to her mother in tears after the Japanese assistant had fled the news of her pregnancy. Celine had let her cry, watching her from across the kitchen table. She had said, I know, I know. Poor girl. Poor girl. And Sumin had cried more, wanting the attention to last. And then Celine had said, But really, Sumin, what did you expect? You must know, she had said, what kinds of consequences this kind of behavior has. And then she expressed regret at losing a competent assistant.

Sumin couldn't even remember how the decision to have the baby had been arrived at. She couldn't remember whether her mother had expressed an opinion. She remembered that it had always just seemed like having the baby was what she would do.

Through the second book, and then the third, Sumin watched and listened during the shoots as if the Captain's presence on the deck kept the ship from sinking. "Hold still," she heard over and over until she steadied herself, pretending her mother was talking to

75

her. And if Cam couldn't stay still, and Celine stepped back away from her camera, it was Sumin's small groan that everyone heard, her failure across her face like heat.

And she'd steal away, or be sent away. And when Cam, her face wet with wiped-away tears, climbed the stairs afterwards to her mother's room, where her mother was waiting, Sumin would ask, What? And Cam would look at her and Sumin would say something like, Come on, come on, knowing that she wanted the tears to stop more for her own sake than for her daughter's.

And here was her daughter now, grown-up and tan with her own little girl. The old independence and self-reliance. Unwilling, as usual, to let her mother in on any of her intimate thoughts. The poise didn't come from Sumin, but it came from her decisions. Wasn't that the same thing?

Alice shook the open box of Roll-Ups and they flew all over the car.

"Great," Cam said.

For Sumin, the question always had been: How can I help her be more of a person than I am? But she'd always known that the current flowed the other way; the current that passed between Celine and Cam—she received some of it, like waves. She glanced at Alice in the rearview mirror. And you, she thought. What do you receive, and at whose expense?

My father showed me my first camera. It remains the briefest of memories. A thirteen-by-eighteen on a tripod. It had a dark focusing cloth. The photographer's hand manipulated the focus, pulled off the lens cap to expose the image, and after a count to three, put it back.

My mother gave me my first one after we moved to Paris. An odd gift, everyone noted, but my father approved. In Paris at the time, technical knowledge in any one subject never sufficed as a mark of success. My doctor father had cultivated a genuine interest in the arts and letters. He had an extensive collection: Monet, Pissarro, Sisley, Degas and, of course, Picasso. He even painted a little himself.

The camera was meant to make up for the upheaval in my life. Rosewood veneer. The focusing glass was taken up and out of the top through open doors, and the plateholder slid down into its place. The doors were hinged to open one towards the front, the other towards the back, each with a little knob of bone. Two other knobs, like tiny doorstops, were set into the top of the box upon which the knobs of the door struck. At any time, night or day, I could hear the sound those small circles of bone made against each other. I opened and closed them countless times.

The odor of iodine from the coated plates. I thought the box was the body and the lens was the soul, with the gift of carrying the image to the plate. I stopped resenting having to learn French when I discovered that their word for lens was *l'objectif*.

I learned about cameras and pictures in French. I had only what I read. At the beginning, I made ridiculous errors—the room was not dark enough, the time was not long enough—but slowly I discovered how everything worked.

After my family went to bed I went to work. I uncovered things I would not share with them. I achieved solitude.

Easing my head under the focusing cloth was a thrill. To pivot the camera slowly around, watching the image change on the ground glass, was a revelation. Tableaux passed across the milky rectangle. I was a discoverer of things no one else had seen.

And no matter how good the picture was, the one I had in mind was better. There was, I came to realize there had to be, a level of frustration at all times. The shots you achieved you took for granted. The shots you lost you never forgot.

We'd been in Paris a week when a cousin, a few years older, explained why she'd been staring at my mother. The schoolchildren had been saving the silver paper from their chocolate bars to roll into large silver balls. The balls were then given to the Sisters of Charity to be sold to buy back the soul of a little Chinese girl. My cousin had been convinced that my mother was the result of this sale.

I vented such humiliations onto my mother. I stopped answering to my Chinese name. I

78

mocked her attempts to pronounce my French one. It became my goal to move her out of the way.

Overcoming her became the equivalent of learning European table manners or fluent French.

And I learned all those things to be able to maneuver in a variety of venues. Today I shall be the tall, exotic Asian. Tomorrow I shall be the cultured Frenchwoman. The next day, something else. Whatever was called for, whatever worked.

My father was appalled by this behavior. He spoke to me, with love, about the danger of making one's sense of right and wrong too flexible. He spoke of the importance of knowing how to behave under the least dignified circumstances. I told him I understood, and did nothing to alter my behavior, except to try and keep it from his watchful eye.

The design with Cam was to cause accidents. Have her show what she preferred to conceal: the revelation of the gargoyle in us all. Those first great fractures of fear when she knew that life would entail much pain.

⟍⟋

*T*hey came upon Berryville, not Flint Hill, which was nowhere near where they wanted to be.

"We *are* lost," Alice announced, peering out her tiny window.

Cam studied the map and said, "I wonder

79

how that happened." Sumin suggested that if Cam had done less talking and more navigating, they wouldn't have gotten into this position.

Cam then mentioned that she'd talked to Celine about Grady.

"I like Grady," Alice said.

The guy in the car behind them was shaking his fist at the woman next to him. The woman was slumped in her seat, her arms crossed.

"So," Sumin said. "And?"

Cam rummaged in her bag. She unearthed some gum. "And nothing. She asked what I thought of him."

Alice leaned forward. "What are you eating?" she asked.

Cam opened her mouth wide and showed Alice the wad of gum.

"Oh," Alice said, and remained leaning forward.

Cam glanced up at the road. "Try to stay between the lines, Mother."

Sumin swerved the wheel back and forth. The angry guy honked.

"Whoa," Alice said.

"Very nice," Cam said.

"Is that gum?" Alice asked.

Cam rummaged around in her bag again and passed a piece back.

"What did you tell her?" Sumin asked.

Cam blew a bubble and sucked it back in before it could pop.

Sumin looked at her.

Cam said, "I don't see him all that much, you know."

They passed a church Sumin had never seen before. "Do you recognize any of this?" she asked, looking down at the map as if she could read it from the driver's seat.

Cam looked ahead. "Nope."

The angry guy passed them on the left. Cam watched. "Those two looked happy," she said.

"Where?" Alice said.

"Missed it," Cam said.

"What did she say?" Sumin said, persevering.

"Relax," Cam said. "How much older he is. He only has one book." She looked at her mother. "You've heard it all before."

They were both quiet. Sumin thought of Grady's birthday a few months ago. His sixty-fifth. They had celebrated by going to a movie and buying him a senior ticket. Sumin reached for a cigarette and held it, unlit, with the hand that was steering.

"Thought you'd quit," Cam said.

"It's not lit," Sumin said. She rolled the cigarette on her thigh with her free hand.

She popped the lighter and lit the cigarette. Cam rolled down her window and sighed loudly. Sumin opened her own and switched the cigarette to her other hand. Outside noise filled the car.

Cam said, "What time is it? Seems like we should've gotten there by now."

"We're *lost*," her mother reminded her.

"We're *lost*," Alice echoed.

Cam lifted her face to the falling sun. The

wind was blowing her hair all over the place. She seemed not to notice.

"What does that mean—'he only has one book'?" Sumin finally asked. "He isn't that smart?"

Cam didn't say anything.

"Did she say that?" Sumin asked. "Those words?"

Cam gave her a look.

"She's only met him something like three times," Sumin said. "*You* don't even really know him."

Cam rolled up the window and cleared her throat.

The sun rolled on to their right.

Sumin threw her cigarette out and pushed her oversized sunglasses up the bridge of her nose. "Well," she said bitterly. "What can we do about Celine. Sometimes she's a total jerk, right?"

Cam looked down, like she was embarrassed, and Sumin realized she was, for her mother, and suddenly she didn't want to be in the car with her daughter.

"Are we still lost?" Alice asked.

"There aren't many people she thinks are worth anything," Cam said quietly.

Her attempt to help made Sumin even angrier, and she pulled over, to throw her daughter and Alice out of the car, hand them the portrait, wave sayonara, and not even look back in the rearview mirror.

We would be descending soon and I couldn't stand it any longer. I headed back up the aisle.

Hsing Chiang was asleep, her hands on her bundle of knitting. I stood over her for a moment. Finally, her seatmate looked up and said, "She's asleep."

I retreated to the back of the plane.

A man in the back row whose clothes all advertised something called the Redskins was trying to load his camera. A point-and-shoot. The names of the late nineteenth-century mass-produced hand cameras came back: Escopette—Pistol; PDQ—Photography Done Quickly; Hit-or-Missit.

The first letter I received from my parents after Paris had been occupied related that by the end of that first afternoon, the German soldiers were all out taking photos of the sights.

When she was about Alice's age, I tried to teach Sumin how to use a camera. I gave her my four-by-five and told her to disassemble it, assemble it. I told her to unscrew every screw and find out herself what to do with it. You mustn't treat a child as a nitwit. It took her over an hour to remove the holding knob. Finally I took it away.

The Redskin was on his third try. It was painful to watch. I moved back down the aisle. Hsing Chiang was still asleep.

Back in my seat, I allowed myself certain questions: Had I underestimated this Grady?

His previous articles that I'd seen, the one on Contemporary Chinese artists, the other on Chinese filmmakers, had been fine—workmanlike, risk-free. What could this woman have told him?

These led to others. When was the last time I had loaded a camera? How large a mistake had it been, agreeing to do the photos for this article? What was it about the little girl that was pushing at me? Why did I care?

I reached beneath the seat for my camera bag. It was newer than the camera. I once had a heavy metal case with reinforced edges and corners. Before that, a wicker suitcase.

Now, black nylon. I found the zipper and unzipped enough for my hand to work its way around the curves and angles of the machine inside. Stieglitz used an eight-by-ten view camera, its sagging bellows held up by string and adhesive tape.

Even folded, the Toyo gave up its worn spots and nicks. It was just a box really, half a foot wide. Twisting my fingers awkwardly, I outlined the collapsed bellows. Old lovers, warming themselves on nostalgia. There had been no big moment, no dramatic announcements when the Cam photos stopped. A new self-consciousness had crept into her movements; the woman-child had given way to more woman, less child, and the photos just stopped. And, now, my breathing evened, the dizziness receded. For the time being I had succeeded in grasping confidence and holding it with the intensity necessary to be convincing.

❧

UNTITLED

A YOUNG GIRL, naked, lying upside down across the middle of a bed. To the right a door, opened onto a darkened hallway. A chenille bedspread is made beneath her. A window above her head washes her body with light.

Her back is bent over the edge of the bed. Her head hangs upside down, her hair pooling on the floor. Her eyes are open.

Next to her, the pages of a letter and a torn envelope, all in disarray.

❧

Nobody had thrown anybody out. They'd sat there for a while, cars going by every now and then, until Alice had said, "What are we doing?" and Cam had suggested that perhaps Sumin needed a break from driving. At that Sumin had snatched the map from beneath her daughter's feet, consulted it for a minute, and pulled back onto the road.

Alice had asked where they were going now.

They hit a bird about ten minutes after that. They surprised a whole flock of the sort of dust-colored pigeons that Alice had been demanding they look at every few miles for the

85

last hour. One made the wrong choice and flew dead-on off the windshield.

Cam shrieked. Sumin swerved. The car skidded to the gravel shoulder. The bird was long gone over the top.

"What?" Alice kept asking. "What?"

"Shit," Sumin said, sitting there, staring at the windshield. There was one crack.

Cam was out of the car, pacing. She shook her hands as if to get feeling back in them. Alice scrambled out after her and started turning in circles, looking at the ground. "Where is it?" she asked. "What did we hit?" She stopped turning suddenly and looked up at Cam. "Was it a person?" she said quietly, as if she didn't want to jinx her possible good fortune.

"Are you alright?" Cam asked.

Alice looked at her like she couldn't believe how completely Cam had missed the point.

Sumin got out too and found herself scanning the hedges and brush lining the two-lane road. She asked Cam if she was alright.

Cam nodded, but said, "Jesus. Did you see that?"

Alice had climbed up the front of the car to examine the windshield. No one told her to get off.

Sumin circled behind the car. The bird was in the road behind them. One wing was spread out at an odd angle, and it was trying to walk. Its head made pecking motions towards the side of the road. Wait until Cam saw this.

She glanced up and down the road. It was deserted. Cam came up behind her. "Oh, shit," she said, bending her knees. "It's still alive."

"I see that," Sumin said.

They both stared at it, like the ball was in its court.

Alice's voice came from the hood of the car. "Where's the blood?" she asked.

"Come on," Cam said, turning and walking back to the car. "Let's go before she sees it." She took Alice by the hand and helped her jump off the car. She tried to get her to get back in the car. "No way," Alice said, twisting to get free. Sumin hadn't moved. "Sumin," Cam called. "Come on." The imperiousness had returned to her voice.

This is what passes for mercy with my daughter, Sumin thought.

Alice broke away from Cam and ran back to join Sumin. She stared at the bird. "I'll get a box," she said. "We'll take it to the animal doctor."

Sumin shook her head. "We can't save this one," she said.

Alice stared at her. "I'll get a box," she said again. She turned and ran back to the car.

Sumin squatted. Her sunglasses fell onto the bird, and she snatched them away. Cam was looking back at her. Alice was rummaging around in the backseat. The bird recovered from the sunglasses and cocked its head to keep her in its view. There was a little blood. Sumin reached down and cupped its body with one hand. With the other she found its head. It

87

seemed to recognize her help. She closed her eyes and her grip simultaneously and twisted, and then she rose and met Cam's stare, both of them sick and surprised at her action. This is what passes for mercy with me, she thought.

They told Alice the bird had died. She spent the rest of the ride on her knees in the backseat, staring out of the rear window, refusing to talk to them.

The initial descent of the plane urged me forward. What was left of the older woman's drink across the aisle slopped onto her shoes.

Children. How had photographers like Cameron accomplished what they had with all those children around them? The parent had rights too: the right to rest, to silence, to work undisturbed. Cam had possessed almost no work discipline before this child. There would be less than none now.

There were ways, of course, of dealing with children. I appealed above all to their capacity for comprehension.

I quoted Colette: Touch what you please. Enter into contact with everything around you. If you want to drink out of that beautiful Chinese teacup, do so, but know that if you break it, you will forever deprive yourself of drinking from it again.

I told them to take care. The wasp had a sting, but whether they got stung or not, when all was said and done, was their business.

Perhaps this little girl would have sense.

Knives cut, pliers pinched: reasons for learning how to put both to their proper uses. And when they weren't put to proper use, I told them: You are bleeding. Next time, handle yourself more suitably.

Monday

Sumin was up and downstairs before anyone. Alice hadn't slept well. It had taken Cam over an hour to get her to sleep, and then a few hours later, Sumin had heard loud, gulping sobs coming from their room. She'd finally gone to check on them, pushing their door open just slightly. Cam was curled on her side on top of the covers. Alice was kneeling over her, patting her head. Cam's crying was making the bed shake, and the girl rocked with its movements. Every now and then Alice would lean over, put her face against Cam's and say, "Don't be sad." Sumin backed away from the door without closing it. The sobs had continued off and on throughout the night.

She washed the dishes from the night before. Alice's Cookie Monster cup—it was some kind of security object. Her mother had bought it when they first came to the States, and had told her that drinking lukewarm tea from it before she went to sleep would keep the bad dreams away. Dream tea, Alice called it. Celine's tea mug, Cam's wineglass with her lip prints circling the rim. She wore that lip balm stuff that came in a little tub. When she found out that it might be carcinogenic, she took to offering it to people more often, saying, "Cancer anyone?"

Cam's desperation the night before had been disarming. Sumin realized she should be worried, but all she kept coming back to was how unwilling Cam was to ever talk about anything. What each of them wanted out of this week seemed too complicated to work out to everyone's satisfaction. The familiar sense that she would get the short end of the stick gave her a knot in her stomach. As did the recurring images of Cam sobbing in bed. Sumin could just manage to get her mind around a mildly sad Cam, but last night had been something else. Why should Cam be so unhappy? And Alice's reactions had communicated familiarity; she was used to this role.

She made everything worse by thinking about the car conversation. Now she could think of a million ways she might have picked up on things her daughter had been talking about. "Six and Sixty," for example—the photo of Cam and the farmer from the next place over eating berries—that was a perfect example of the lighting effect Cam had wanted to talk about.

That day Sumin had known that they were probably late for the shoot, but Cam had said yes to picking blackberries out by the pond, and that didn't happen very often even then. Their fingers had been stained and they'd had berry seeds between their teeth. When they'd returned, Celine was on the porch.

Celine had been charming because the farmer was there. She liked being liked by the locals. She'd taken the bowl of berries out of Sumin's hand to use in the shoot. She'd had Cam and the guy stand with their backs to each other, the width of the frame between them, each with a berry between their lips. In the print, Cam's lips are stained, and the upper half of her face is lightened away. The farmer's face is sharp and dark, his mouth just nearing the edge of the frame.

During the shoot Sumin had been mortified, as if this had been her fault.

The farmer had been full of admiration for something he hadn't even understood. In Celine, and in six-year-old Cam.

Sumin dried her hands. She stood in the middle of the kitchen, looking around. Maybe Alice would like to go berry picking.

The big moment of Celine's arrival had been deflating. She'd barely acknowledged Alice, though Cam kept steering the little girl by the shoulders into her line of vision. At one point, the three of them had been unable to avoid one another in the center of the room and had seemed like some kind of per-formance-art piece. Celine had closed her eyes until Cam had backed Alice away to sit with her in the one of the wingback chairs.

Celine had been unimpressed with the cleaning woman's work. She'd rearranged the cattails Cam had dumped in the copper jar in the breezeway. She'd ordered a cup of tea and had frowned at the mug. She'd said she was tired and had gone up to her room for the rest of the night.

Well, Sumin thought impatiently, what had I expected? Group hugs? Tears? A nostalgic tour of the cabin, all three of them holding hands?

It annoyed her to no end that despite reams of evidence, she still expected more. The one and only psychiatrist she had tried had suggested that she work on just not being depressed.

Alice had watched Celine go up the stairs, a small furrow in her brow, and then had complained that no one had told her that Celine had *short* hair.

At nine, Sumin drove to the store for the paper. On the way back, she passed the stable at the end of their road. Yesterday, on the drive in, she'd noticed Alice lingering on the two bays in the front paddock, craning her neck to keep them in sight as long as she could. The sign said: lessons for all ages. She stopped and wrote the number. When she came back, they were still asleep. She put the kettle on. She made oatmeal. Kids liked oatmeal, right? She waited for them to wake up, for the day to start.

It was disconcerting how quickly she'd slipped back into the routine. Even the smells were disarmingly familiar: the pine floor, the mustiness of a closed-up house, the cleaning woman's Murphy's Oil.

She found it completely believable that she hadn't changed at all in twelve years. Alice's presence encouraged that sense.

At nine-thirty, Cam and Alice came downstairs holding hands. They waved and walked over to the pot on the stove. Cam lifted the lid and peered down. "Oatmeal?" she said. "In the middle of July?" She didn't look like she'd spent the night crying.

"Try it before you crab about it," Sumin said, thinking she should've made corn bread.

"I want a waffle," Alice said.

Cam cursed. Apparently, the only thing Alice would eat in the morning was a single plain waffle. No syrup. Cam looked at her mother. "Could you?" she said.

"Could I what?" Sumin said.

Cam gestured towards Alice. "Could you get her a waffle?"

Sumin gestured towards the newspaper. "I've already been to the store," she said.

Cam put her hand on Alice's head. "Sumin won't go to the store for you," she said.

Alice's eyes filled with tears.

Cam smoothed Alice's hair behind her ears. "Don't cry, silly. I'll go."

Cam was wearing a long hot-pink tank top that said *Santa Clara Beach Club* in teal. A palm tree waved across the letters. She grabbed the keys off the kitchen table and asked Alice if she wanted to come. Alice shook her head, found a pen and some scrap paper and settled on the floor to draw.

"You're going out in that?" Sumin asked.

Cam held it out from her body as if seeing it for the first time. She smoothed the shirt flat over her stomach. She was not wearing a bra.

"It's a little late to start worrying about the world seeing my nipples," she said flatly.

"Go get your daughter her waffles," Sumin said.

Alice looked up instantly. "I'm not her daughter," she said. "I have a mother," she said.

Cam squatted to kiss her. "Of course you do," she said. She lowered her voice. "Sumin is a little..." She twirled a finger by her temple and crossed her eyes.

Alice smiled to herself and told her to hurry up.

Sumin followed Cam outside. She stood by the door watching her daughter walk to the car.

Cam looked up. "What?" she said.

Sumin started to speak, then stopped.

Cam sighed and opened the car door.

Sumin said, "I saw you last night."

Cam looked instantly sad.

"Are you okay?" Sumin said.

Sumin's concern seemed to make Cam feel worse.

"I don't know," she said. She seemed on the verge of tears again. "What if Celine doesn't get what a good thing Alice is for me?"

Sumin was at a loss. Cam got in the car.

Alice called from inside the house. She needed more paper. Cam drove away and Sumin called to the receding car, "Don't be sad."

While Cam was gone, Alice drew. She drew horses and tractors with drivers who looked suspiciously like herself. Sumin pretended to read the paper, and watched. Alice worried her upper lip with her tongue as she drew. She sat on her knees, bent close to the paper, like a nearsighted Japanese woman, the whole time. Her hair fell across her paper.

Sumin thought about asking Alice about last night. And then felt asking a six-year-old for reassurance was too pathetic even for her.

Finally Alice sat up and surveyed her work. Sumin got ready to field a question about when she could drive a tractor.

"How many is my mother away?" she asked.

"What do you mean?" Sumin asked, though she knew what she meant.

Alice looked around the room, as if trying to find the right way to ask. "When do I go to her house again?"

Sumin didn't know what to say. She knelt next to her, and they both stared at the drawings. "What does Cam say?" she asked.

Alice sat cross-legged. Their knees touched. "She says my mother is working on it, but it's hard work and it might take a long time." She was quiet for a moment. "How long is a long time?" she asked.

Sumin said she didn't know.

They were both quiet. The birds outside seemed to have gotten louder.

Alice touched Sumin's chin. "But Celine can make it a shorter time."

God, Sumin thought. What are you doing with us? She wanted to gather the little girl in her lap, and tell her she was sorry, but this family couldn't offer that kind of help. It was beyond them.

As if reading her mind, Alice stood up and said she was going out.

❧

𝒩o sleep again.

I couldn't hold the plane trip fully responsible. What was it about the child? Was it as obvious as the parallels with Cam?

Why? Cam had asked on the phone when I told her I was arranging for the child's return to China. Why are you so interested? Why do you care where she lives? Can you not let me have anything of my own?

I'd had no answers for her. Only the slightly shameful certainty that neither her nor the child's best wishes were at the heart of my concern.

❧

𝒜lice ate her waffle in silence; Cam hunted around the fruit bowl. She touched every peach and then started in on the plums. When she was done, she moved to the cupboards. She open and shut doors. "God," she said. "Didn't we get anything at the grocery store?"

Alice looked up. "Yeah," she said. "Fruit Roll-Ups."

Even Cam laughed.

She suggested a walk down to the honeysuckle. Alice agreed, mildly interested. "I haven't seen any horses," she said, putting on her shoes.

It took Sumin a minute to realize the invitation didn't include her. She fingered the stable's phone number in her pocket. Cam went upstairs to change into shorts and a bathing-suit top. Then she slathered Alice with sunscreen and bug spray; Sumin sipped her tea and realized she wouldn't have thought of either. She watched them head across the back meadow, resentful and relieved.

Once, when Cam was six, it had been dark and Sumin had thought she was in her room. She hadn't been, and Sumin had gone back downstairs to lean over the porch railing and call her. She'd stood there straining to see past the illuminated part of the backyard into the darkness and the fields. She hadn't even been able to remember what her daughter had been wearing.

After letting her call for a while, Celine had come out, holding a glass of iced tea. "She's down in the field," she'd remarked. "In the honeysuckle."

"What honeysuckle?" was all Sumin had been able to say.

Hours later, Cam had come back on her own. The next morning Sumin had made Celine take her there. Cam had carved tunnel after tunnel through it.

"She's always gone here," Celine had said. "For years."

So Sumin had resolved not to always fret about her. She was making some place for herself; she would be back. Instead, she'd concentrated on what to do on her own in the meantime.

It was eleven, and Celine was still upstairs, no sounds. Unheard-of for her, even with jet lag.

Cam had remarked the night before how she'd seemed a little off. She'd rested before her inspection of the cabin. Neither of them had seen that before. She'd been quiet for long periods of time. She'd looked old.

Back during her mother's late work nights, Sumin left Celine's dinner covered with a plate on the dining-room table. She left beside it a flower, a piece of fruit, or a drawing she'd made that day while waiting.

The tokens had been like the letters Cam had sometimes written her. She'd wrap them in her mother's napkin for Sumin to discover at breakfast.

"So we weren't total monsters," Sumin said aloud to the empty kitchen.

At eleven-twenty, Sumin crept up the stairs, trying to remember and skip the ones that creaked, and peeked into her mother's room.

She was in bed, her sheet stretched tightly across her chest, her arms at her sides. Her eyes were shut, and she was biting her bottom lip.

Sumin should've gone in, but she'd been trained to hover. Just walk right in? As Cam would say, "Not really you, huh?"

It was the way Sumin used to stand outside Celine's darkroom, like a mother outside a baby's room, straining to hear.

During *Six* she'd found them once down by the honeysuckle tunnels. Cam had been wearing only a jacket from a Red Guard uniform, and when Sumin had arrived Celine had asked her granddaughter to spread her legs. Sumin's murmur had been audible. She had been thinking of what to say in protest, but Celine had turned and said, "This is it, no? This is the complete picture." And Sumin had worked to puzzle through the comment while the shoot had continued.

Those summers had been a series of incidents in which she'd let her daughter down. At the beginning of each summer, she'd stood in the upstairs hall watching her mother unpack her daughter's bag. Her mother had looked at each T-shirt, each dress like a nun who'd renounced all earthly goods. Each time Sumin had just stood there, her arms electric with goose bumps, and then she'd walked away.

That was her life, she thought now, with aggravation: hovering in hallways. She told herself it was jet lag and left her mother lying there.

She returned downstairs without any attempt at quiet.

She got more tea and went to sit in one of the director's chairs on the porch. It was already hot, and she found the breeziest part of the deck, propping her feet up on the railing. If someone looked up and saw her, she thought, they'd think she was pretty lucky.

Grady'd be there by evening. Maybe she'd still be sitting here.

She tried to think of ways to help her daughter this time. Could she convince Celine that Alice was better off with Cam? Not likely. She couldn't convince herself, and even if she could, she carried what you might call very little authority with Celine. Passivity was her realm of expertise, she thought dismally.

At the party to celebrate one of Celine's first successes, she'd been eight or nine and had been called on to recite the Chinese poem that had inspired her mother's latest series. Celine had coached her.

She'd stood at one end of the living room, knowing there were only one or two grown-ups who'd even understand if she made a mistake.

When she was done, amidst the applause, Celine had patted the seat next to hers. She'd adjusted Sumin's skirt, rearranged her hair and talked to everyone but Sumin. And in her need to have company in her embarrassment, Sumin had shrugged her mother's hand away. She'd stood up and sat back down, doing her own rearranging. That had been all it took: Celine had taken her daughter by the hand down the hallway to her darkroom, saying she'd unlock the door when Sumin could behave like an adult.

Sumin had listened to the party noise. She had smelled her mother's chemicals and the lingering odor of her aloe soap. She had looked over the metal trays and the clothes-lines spider-webbing the room with strips of negatives and prints hanging from them.

There were typed labels on the backs of prints, across the edges of trays and around the brown glass bottles.

She'd cut everything cuttable into small, thin shreds.

By the time the others had left, and Celine had tidied up and walked past the locked door two or three times, Sumin had destroyed the room.

Years later, Celine had interpreted the story to her granddaughter as the best indication of true disturbance in Sumin.

Cam had passed this on to Sumin, and Sumin had enjoyed the image of her mother and daughter as potentially shocked by Sumin's capacity for instability.

But despite the pleasure moments of action gave her, she found it near impossible to perform them. "You're pathetic," she said into her mug. She pitched the remaining tea over the rail. The breeze caught it and sprayed her feet. "Perfect," she said, making no move to wipe herself off.

She sat on the porch and tried to concentrate on a field filled with the kind of sunshine that was too bright to look at. But the backs of her calves had fallen asleep against the railing, and the morning breeze had evaporated before the approaching midday stillness. And Alice's questions kept coming back to her. She felt as if what was facing her from then on was a vast, congested, overlit space.

———

don't revel in nostalgia. Still, there was pleasure in waking up here. A life without shoes. I vaguely recalled crying from last night. My imagination?

I'd sat up, and had felt light-headed with a twinge in my lower back. The same feeling Steven Liu had provoked. The pull of my body, keeping me from what I wanted to do.

It took father years to convince mother to use Western medicine. "Would I hurt you?" he would argue, and she would half-close her eyes, pretending she had not heard the question.

Her Chinese tonic was usually a brew of wine, herbs and ground shells that she refused to identify.

I cannot think of my father without thinking of that sad odor of medicine that clung to his clothes from the hospital.

When I was a child, my father told me that in churches with stained-glass windows, flies would never pass through the violet and blue rays. He repeated the line in one of his letters during the war. I hadn't known what to make of it. Was it code? I remembered still almost every detail I learned from those letters. The first day of Occupation, and the clouds of black soot from the burning petrol reserves in the suburbs. An absence of birds until autumn. The sign on the door of Le Chabanais, the most famous brothel in Paris: THE ESTABLISHMENT WILL REOPEN AT THREE O'CLOCK.

Private cars, buses, taxis remained garaged for four years. *We hear things,* my father wrote in 1940, *that we haven't heard in years.* As a doctor, he could've used his car. He chose not to, visiting his private patients by bicycle, his valet following behind, balancing the doctor's bag on his own bicycle.

Later, the streetlamps were painted blue, requiring the use of flashlights, also with a blue filter. In the mornings, children gathered shrapnel on the lawns of the Jardin de Luxembourg. At the Casino de Paris, girls with tricolor feathers on their bottoms sang, *"Ça sent si bon la France"*—"France smells so good"—to their audience of Germans.

My father's personal fortune and contacts in the country allowed almost full larders and quiet resistance. He shook hands with strangers wearing the yellow star. He congratulated his friend, Judge Didier, on refusing to take the oath of loyalty to Pétain. And yet, my father was invited to the most brilliant parties Paris had seen in years.

In May of 1944, the Germans inexplicably requisitioned all dogs over eighteen inches at the shoulder. My father guessed that they would be used to run under tanks with bombs on their backs. By the end of June, collaborators had received miniature coffins and death notices in red ink in the mail.

And the letters after the Liberation, urging me to visit as soon as possible, reminding me that my mother hadn't seen me in years, asking why I had not responded to his last letter.

I imagined Hsing Chiang's reunion with her sister.

Sumin downstairs and then outside my door. I wished I'd locked it. Keeping the cabin small had meant no way of disappearing. In my parents' houses in Shanghai and Paris, I could separate myself from others for hours on end.

Here I heard everything. The bickering had started. Something about oatmeal. Where was the child during all this? If she was like me, or my mother, she was pulling herself above it, making herself quiet and dignified, an artifact on a high shelf.

When I went downstairs, there were her drawings. Surprisingly good. The horses depicted various gaits, and she'd done an admirable job with perspective. I folded one and put it in my pocket, and spent a few minutes watching two cats through the side window. Perhaps related to one of the old ones. Could any still have been alive? These were a rust-colored shorthair and her almost-grown kitten. She gave it continued blows to the head. The kitten pawed back.

I went out onto the porch and sat. The cats took an interest.

Sumin was already there. She dragged her chair closer; I could smell her.

"It's Nivea," she said.

"Was I sniffing?" I asked.

"You were sniffing," she said.

She had remarked long ago that part of what drew me to Cam was fear. She'd added that if she'd been able to scare me, I would've

106

paid more attention to her. I told her that I was under the impression that I'd paid quite a bit of attention to her. "Good for you," she'd answered.

What had made me think of that?

"Hot," Sumin said, stretching her legs out in front of her.

"Yes," I said. "Summer after summer." It was beautiful weather: a warmth so imperious and gentle that it was a form of grace. As always, there was value in making people believe they'd been allowed to share something, even when they hadn't.

I'd always told Sumin that Cam was filled with secrets and that I could capture them. Everyone was excited by a little disclosure.

From the porch I could see the studio's small front door. Cam and I had painted it white. You had to stoop to enter. Alice would like it. Cam had.

The tiny paned windows were champions at letting in light. In summer we filled the fireplace with flowers. There were few books. In a bookstore I'd browse, but I didn't need those people in my home.

After work I'd have a sandwich and tea in one of my China Blue chairs. After hours in the darkroom, my legs were swollen from standing. I'd collapse into bed, the adrenaline coursing through me.

I'd meant to go over there this morning. I hadn't been in there for twelve years. Who knew what the caretaker and the cleaning woman had wrought.

Camera obscura—literally, the darkroom.

At first, I hadn't used the studio much. One of my earliest shots had been the side of a cliff face. I'd clung to the sheer slope for the composition, braced myself without my hands while focusing. The knowledge that I was now incapable of that lapped at me like an agitated dog. I experienced a completely fabricated image of Alice bending over her drawings.

I might've begun my art to see something I had the vague sense that I'd forgotten. And then with Cam, the familiar was made new.

I heard Sumin say, "What?"

I looked at her.

"You said something," she said.

"Did I?" The willow over the pond was still except for the tips of its branches, which seemed to be trying to inspire a breeze by themselves. The water was greenish-black beneath. The afternoon of a shoot by the edge of the pond when Cam was twelve, the water had been jade green and tranquil, and we'd slipped in—Cam in the silk pajamas and myself in my sundress.

Sumin put her feet up on the railing and sighed. "Maybe if I had some kind of guide," she said. "*The Blue Guide to Celine*."

I was getting bored. I blamed her. Where were Cam and Alice? She wasn't going to convince me to let her keep Alice by disappearing all the time. Horses were leaving the back field. Nearer to the porch, two chaffinches quarreled on a branch and flew to the ground.

For Sumin there would never be the knowledge of what it was to be desperate over an image. There was no passion, no unadulterated dedication. To anything. All she knew of those summers was dips in the pond, naps in the sun. So instead, I said, "I have no rules. Especially not for you."

"What's that supposed to mean?" she asked. "What do you mean, especially not for me?"

I got up. "Please," I said.

"Where are you going?"

"Away," I said.

"Wait," she said, not looking at me. "I want to ask you something."

I picked up my teacup and started towards the kitchen door. I reminded her that I'd told her a thousand times what was wrong with her life.

She said nothing, as expected, and once in the house I slid the door shut behind me.

❧

UNTITLED

A WOMAN AND a baby lying in the grass by a pond. The woman is on her back. The baby is on her stomach. Their wet swimsuits lie in a heap in the upper right corner.

The baby is completely visible. The half of the woman closest to the baby fills the right half of the frame.

The baby's arm reaches up to the woman's breast. She pinches the woman's nipple between tiny fingers. The hair on the woman's arm stands on end.

The entire image looks as if it's submerged under a layer of oil.

❧

$\mathcal{S}$umin *was* still sitting there when Grady arrived. It was late afternoon. Cam and Alice were still gone. Celine was still up in her room. Sumin heard the distinctive sound of his Isuzu and the crunch of tires on the driveway and she was annoyed. As if he were the reason she was still sitting there, no closer to what she wanted.

He called hello three times. He came around the house the long way, not knowing the shortcut through the breezeway. But the sight of him, car-rumpled, made her feel small and embarrassed, and she was silent until he noticed her on the porch.

"Hey," he said. "Didn't you hear me?" He gestured back towards the car. "What happened to the VW?"

She explained about the bird.

He asked if Alice was okay. He asked where Celine was.

The annoyance was back. She shrugged and stood up. "Here I am," she said.

He smiled and crossed the porch to hug her. She inhaled. His shaving cream, the cats, his sweat. Was this going to be worse than she'd imagined? She held her breath and hugged harder.

He pulled away. "Is that the studio?" he asked, leaning out over the railing.

She stood, arms in an unfinished hug, playing an imaginary audience for sympathy.

"Is it?" he asked.

She joined him at the railing. "That's it. The Little House of Miracles."

He didn't respond.

She said she guessed it wasn't the mythic structure he expected.

He turned around and sat on the railing. He took a breath, started to say something, then didn't.

"What?" she said.

He smiled, turning his head to look out over the back meadow and pond. "It's beautiful here, isn't it?"

Cam's voice came up the side stairs. "What did I tell you?" she said.

Alice was quiet.

"You tell me," Cam said. "What did I say?"

Alice mumbled something.

Sumin and Grady turned around. Both girls were wet. Water dripped off the ends of their hair. Alice was hugging herself; despite the heat, goose bumps covered her legs and arms.

"Hey," Grady said, smiling.

"Hey," Alice said, imitating his half-wave. She was suddenly shy and hung back.

Cam said, "Here I am. Let the festivities begin."

Sumin watched her daughter and her lover embrace. The Cam of the night before was a fading image.

"Oh," she said, laughing and pulling away. "I'm getting you soaked."

Grady looked down at his damp shirt. He pulled it away from his chest. He said, "I have to change anyway."

Everyone just stood there.

Cam sat in one of the director's chairs. Grady sat next to her. Sumin stayed where she was.

"Thanks for the gift," Cam said.

Sumin looked at Grady. His "No problem," sounded casual, but he got that pleased face of his.

"The mailman thought I'd sold a portrait," Cam said.

"Sounds like a big gift," Sumin said, the idiot trying to get in on the joke. She thought of the gifts she had brought: a silver bangle in the shape of a snake for Cam, born in the Year of the Snake. A small snapshot of Celine and baby Sumin that Sumin had found stuck into an old journal. She had searched antique store after antique store for the perfect tiny frame, and had been delighted when she found the wooden circle with delicate carvings of rabbits around its face. Celine was born in the Year of the Hare. Now she was sure that both of them would hate the gifts.

Cam looked at her. Clearly she thought her mother knew about Grady's present.

"I bought her some paints," Grady said.

"How nice," Sumin said.

"Yeah," Cam said. "Completely cool."

"I thought they'd be good for the layering you've been trying on the portrait," Grady said.

Does everyone know more about everything than I do? Sumin thought bitterly.

112

Alice was making her way from the top of the stairs to Grady's side. She stole looks at him every so often.

Sumin said, "C'mon, freezing girl. Let's get some dry clothes on."

Alice moved a little closer to Grady. "In a minute," she said. "I'm thinking about some-thing." She glanced at Cam.

Grady laughed and put his arm around her, rubbing her shoulder with his hand.

Sumin took Alice by the hand and led her inside. "Yeah, well, think about things while you change."

Alice stomped her feet and made her hands into little fists, but followed.

Upstairs, they could hear Cam and Grady through the open window. Sumin told Alice to get naked and peered out. She could see the porch roof. Cam's hand stretched out past it, pointing at something in the back field. Prob-ably the honeysuckle caves, Sumin thought. She turned her back on the window.

Alice was still in her wet suit.

"Do you ever feel like mostly, people ignore you, and if they're not ignoring you, they're keeping things from you?" Sumin asked.

Alice said she wanted to call her mother.

Sumin again didn't know what to say. Were they supposed to encourage contact or not? And who paid for what? Did Alice's mother even have a phone? They stared at each other.

"Maybe we can later," she finally said.

Alice got undressed. "That's what Cam

always says." She kicked her wet suit into a corner. "I want to call her now," she said.

"Maybe after dinner," Sumin said, holding her shorts open for her to step into.

Alice grabbed the shorts and threw them across the room. "Not after dinner," she said. "Now."

Her intensity made Sumin hold still. "Cam?" she called, directing her voice out the window.

Alice started crying. She dumped Cam's open suitcase over.

Nine-year-old Cam refusing to take a bath. Sumin had finally had to physically drag her down their apartment hallway to the bathroom. Cam, already tall, had twisted and turned, had braced herself against the wall with both feet and both hands. She succeeded in knocking down almost all of the photos that lined their hallway walls. After they had both calmed down, after the bath, Sumin had made Cam rehang the photos. Now, Sumin couldn't remember why it was so important that Cam take that bath.

Sumin called for her daughter again.

Alice grabbed one of her T-shirts out of the pile and tried to rip it in half. Her face reddened with the effort.

"Cam!" Sumin yelled.

"What?" Cam responded, equaling her mother's impatience.

"You better come up here."

Cam groaned, but a few minutes later appeared in the doorway. In the meantime, Alice had collapsed in the corner on her wet suit.

Her palms beat on the floor. Sumin stood in the opposite corner, watching.

Cam took it all in. "What are you doing?" she said to her mother as she went over to Alice. "Why aren't you helping?"

"How do you help this?" Sumin asked.

Cam lifted Alice into her lap and smoothed the hair from her wet face. Alice gave no indication that she recognized her. She was still crying. Her hands were still moving.

It was the reverse image of the previous night, and Sumin had two thoughts simultaneously: Who are we to keep Cam from this kind of intimacy? How can she shut me out of this kind of intimacy again?

Celine appeared in the doorway. Cam intensified her comforting efforts.

Celine watched for a minute, then crossed the room. She took Alice by the hand and gently told her to stand up. Alice did. Celine put her face close and told her to listen. Alice kept crying. Celine held her face and repeated her command. She asked Alice to find clean clothes. Alice's tears were winding down. She searched through the pile on the floor, and held a sundress out to Celine.

Cam had pulled her knees up to her chest. Sumin couldn't read her face.

Celine pulled the sundress over Alice, and said, "Come. Let's go call your mother. It's early in the morning there; maybe we'll catch her before she starts her day."

Cam stood up. "Celine," she said. "I've already told her we'll call later."

115

Her grandmother ignored her. She turned Alice towards the door.

Cam put her hand on Celine's shoulder. "I said, this has already been decided."

Alice started crying again. "I want to call my mother," she said.

"Of course, dear," Celine said. "We're on our way." They started downstairs.

Cam followed them, calling Celine's name. At the bottom of the stairs, she gave up. "Fine," she said. "Make the call." She reclimbed the stairs. "What do I care what you do?" she said, returning to her room.

Sumin heard Grady ask if everything was okay. She didn't hear Celine's answer. Cam fell onto her bed and stared up at the ceiling, her fingers pressed to her temples.

Sumin watched her. Cam rubbed her eyes with the heels of her hands.

Sumin sat on the bed. "It's just a phone call," she said.

Cam let out a groan. "It's not about the phone call."

"It's not?" Sumin said.

Cam sat up and sat cross-legged the way Alice had earlier. She took her mother's hand. "Listen," she said. "It's not about getting Celine to back off."

Sumin tried to look like she was following.

Cam sighed. "I need her help," she went on. She stared at her mother. "Financially, you know?"

Sumin knew enough to refrain from pointing

out how little Celine liked to part from her money.

Still, she was surprised at the next thing.

"I need your help," Cam said. "Can't you help show her that this is a good thing?" She was beginning to cry.

Every time her daughter cried it was like the first time. The previous night had been the first time she'd seen her like that in years. And still she found herself having the reaction she always had when Cam asked for help. It was the thing she wanted most and the thing she couldn't stand wanting. So it had always been met with a shutting down. Cam had once described it as a disappearing act that allowed Sumin to make her lack of response a matter of couldn't, rather than wouldn't.

The act of calling, just hearing the ringing on the other end, had been enough to make the child feel better. Her mother hadn't been in. I promised her we would try again tomorrow, and we passed some time in my room going over what she would tell her mother about when we did get through.

I put her in my bed, and told her I would sit out on the bedroom deck, right there, where she could see me. Yes, I would stay. Yes, even while she was sleeping.

On the deck the small iron table and chairs were in shadow. The air was still, but something kept me cool. I heard a blackbird, a robin.

She called out in a voice that seemed already asleep. Did her mother miss her?

Yes, I called back. Very, very much.

It was the same question Cam sometimes posed during all those summers. I searched for the appropriate emotional response to the parallels between Cam and Alice and all that appeared were two images: one of Sumin, one of Alice's mother. Sumin had watched me keep Cam to myself and had done nothing but allow it. Her passivity filled me with contempt. How did I feel about this other mother? I didn't yet know.

And then, silence from Alice, and the even breathing of total exhaustion.

That girl in my first school in Paris. Giselle? Camille? Whose parents owned the bookstore by the park. We'd go there after school, once a month. We played cashier, taking turns at ringing up orders for the customers, saying, *"Voici, monsieur." "Merci, madame."*

We didn't talk much. I don't know why we weren't bored with each other sooner.

She stopped inviting me, or I stopped going. One becomes tired of something, and meanwhile an attraction to something else builds. I'm caught between these two things, and they move me along.

Cam cannot handle this child. Even she must admit this.

The cats from earlier this morning were

now on the studio terrace, asleep. Finches flitted over them.

I thought about lying on the chaise. This afternoon's drama had taken its toll. Instead, I took out my notebook and sat at the table. When the article had become a reality, I'd started writing little interviews with myself as way of preempting incompetency. Who better to ask myself questions?

The green pages curled at the corners. There was only one store in Paris that carried these books. The color reminded me of classroom paper. I ordered them a box at a time.

I'd taken to reading the latest entry aloud, as a way of getting started. They were a jumble of prescriptions, from things I never forgot to things I rarely remembered.

Isolate your subject.

Not just recorder, but guide. Educate. Train.

Oliver Wendell Holmes: The very things which an artist would leave out or render imperfectly, the photograph takes infinite [care?] with, and so something something something. What is the picture of a drum without the marks on its head where the beating of the sticks has darkened the parchment?

Cam: what I want the world to mean.

Do what one is not supposed to do.

All relationships have the destructive in them.

And the entry from six months ago, when Cam first told me about Alice. A snippet from a Lewis Carroll poem: *"Do cats eat bats...Do bats eat cats?"*

My first school in Paris had a bare courtyard covered with gravel. There was a single tree. High walls, around which we twelve-year-olds marched in single file, in black jumpers and lace-up shoes.

Recitations. I dreaded and wished for them.

The little girls called me the *Bête Jaune*.

I recited the lessons I'd spent hours over the night before. The words came out exactly as they were supposed to, and when I was done, the teacher always said, "Very nice. I will give you ten out of ten."

Ten out of ten had its own kind of power, and I took my time sitting back down, wrapped in the silence I'd created.

In that silence I came back to Virginia.

A wagtail flew past. Black breast, black cap. It bobbed its tail at me. I went back inside and stood over the sleeping child. Her eyes fluttered beneath their lids. I stood there and stood there, more rested than if I'd been lying on a feather bed. I'd returned to a place not where I belonged, but where, for the moment, I felt familiar and relatively safe.

***

Wandering around the fields out of sight of the cabin, she thought, it wasn't like she hadn't tried. It wasn't like she'd just handed her daughter over and said, Here, do what you want. After a while you begin to catch on to the futility of the effort, and quitting becomes the only thing to do. And who was to say that you couldn't escape, even grow, through submission?

She watched the bottoms of the hedgerows for rabbits or a fox. Late afternoon: it was the best part of the day. The rest of the week came to her clearly: she'd run errands, and the days would go by, and she'd spend nights wondering which way to turn and where to begin or what she was even talking about.

～

    I lowered myself onto the bed next to the child and tried to match my breathing to hers.

Near the end of our first week in Paris, my mother spent an hour dressing me just so and then led me out into the streets. We took a taxi north, to the Parc des Buttes-Chaumont. Walking with her was slow; her bound feet prevented anything but the tiniest of steps. We reached a big garden, where what seemed like hundreds of children were playing undecipherable games.

"Go on," my mother said in Chinese. "Join them."

I refused. She suggested we sit by the garden's edge. I refused that, too, though I knew she needed the rest. We walked back home. And all the way she was not angry with me; I was angry with her. I blamed her with as much venom as I could muster for being Chinese and for being my mother.

What does Cam do with her anger besides snipe at Sumin?

And this child? What must she think of her mother? And what must she think of us, the people who stand in her way?

⁓◦

Dinner was as festive as she'd expected, although Cam and Alice seemed to have recovered, and Grady seemed to have made a decision to ignore the afternoon's dramatics. He hadn't even asked about them.

What am I doing with him? she thought.

After dinner there were presents. Grady went into the kitchen to get Sumin.

"More presents?" she said, closing the refrigerator door. "Do these count as birthday presents, or do I get to sit through more of this on Saturday?"

"Poor Put-Upon Sumin," he said, ushering her back into the dining room.

Telling Grady that she wanted to leave him meant that she didn't get as much mileage out of her Neglected Child routine. She knew she had to get them out of this limbo state; she just didn't know how to decide whether to stay or leave.

The present was a camera. And a tripod. Alice crowded around Celine saying Cam things like: "Cool" and "Lush." Grady pointed out that it was an eight-by-ten Toyo-Field. An updated version of Celine's old one. Cam had no comment. Alice began to fiddle with the tripod.

Sumin sat at her end of the table watching the show. She remembered the old Toyo, the accordian bellows, the tilts, shifts and swings of the front standard.

Her mother was being unusually quiet. During dinner she hadn't shut up.

"Didn't you bring your own camera?" Sumin asked.

Grady answered as if she'd been addressing him. "Who knows what shape that's in," he said. "The magazine wanted to make sure Celine had everything she needed."

Cam suddenly weighed in. "It was a great idea," she said. She got up to attach the new Toyo to the tripod. She showed Alice which screws to turn.

Celine was watching. Her face was tight, like it had been that morning.

"Wasn't this a little expensive?" Sumin asked. Everyone looked at her. She realized how petty she must've sounded.

"Jeez, Sumin," Cam said.

Grady said, "I think they think they'll make their money back."

The phone in the kitchen rang, and Cam went to answer it. Alice wondered if it might be her mother. It was for Grady, someone named Steven Liu. Grady seemed to be expecting the call. He glanced at Celine on his way out of the room.

Alice asked the two women left at the table who Steven Liu was. Neither woman answered, though Sumin waited for her mother to fill her in about yet another person she didn't know.

But Celine didn't seem to be paying attention. This was a different Celine from earlier in the evening.

She'd gone on at some length, rather unexpectedly, on the nutrients necessary for new mothers: poached eggs in raw sugar juice with fermented glutinous rice. For the new baby: cod-liver capsules for skin; fish for the development of the baby's hair.

Cam had wanted to know what this had to do with anything. For some reason it had sent Sumin into a quiet sulk. No one had commented.

Cam had finished setting up the camera. "Come on," she said to Alice. "Ask your great-grandma to take a picture."

Alice lowered her chin. "Stop it," she said. "Stop teasing about that." She got serious. "I don't have to call you those things. I can use your names," she said, as if reciting assembly instructions.

Cam said, "You're right. I'm sorry."

Grady returned, offering no explanations.

Celine sighed. "I wanted isolation. I wanted Cameron and the movements of her beautiful little body."

Cam did a little shimmy.

"Cameron was a beautiful child," Celine said.

Grady couldn't agree fast enough.

Sumin thought, Could this get any more disgusting?

"Not just a record of beauty," Celine said. "The creation of it."

Yes, Sumin thought, it could.

"Are we just forgetting what happened this afternoon?" she asked, despite knowing how ungenerous the comment was.

Alice was snapping her fingers. Celine closed her eyes.

Grady said Sumin's name in a way that asked why she did things like this. She could just hear what he would say to her later: What could you possibly get out of bringing all that up in front of Alice?

Because, Sumin wanted to say in her own defense. Because it was beyond her capacities to make anyone happy.

"We've moved past it," Cam said.

"Apparently," Celine said.

"It wasn't that big a deal," Cam said.

Grady finally asked what happened. No one answered.

Celine rose and went over to the camera. "I used a Rolleiflex for a while, because of the magic of that little mirror in which you could see a smaller version, a marvelous scene."

She ran her fingers around the Toyo. Everyone watched.

"But it became clear it had to be a big camera. A larger negative allowed more detail. One could not, however, get caught up with the historical baggage of the large format. One had to take new kinds of photographs with old equipment."

Cam took her grandmother by the shoulders and maneuvered her behind the camera. "Yeah, yeah, yeah," she said. "Come on." She steered Alice into Celine's vacated chair, and turned back to her grandmother. "Here you go," she said. "Time for 'new kinds of photographs.'"

Grady was examining the scene in front of him. He seemed miles away. The gesture he had made the other night returned to Sumin. What was he turning over in that mind of his?

Alice got out of the chair and sat on the floor.

Celine closed her eyes again. "Nothing offers more difficulty than a smooth, blooming, clean-washed and carefully combed human head."

"You have short hair," Alice said to her.

"Yes, I do," Celine agreed.

"You can't take a picture of my head," Alice said.

"Okay, I won't," Celine said.

"And now," she said to the rest of them. "Now I'm tired. Tomorrow maybe."

Grady snapped out of it. "I thought perhaps we could talk about your plan for the photos," he said.

Celine gave him one of her small smiles. She held out her hand for Alice. "Come," she said. "Time for bed."

Cam didn't comment on the change in sleeping arrangements, but as Alice passed, she did reach out a hand to touch the girl's cheek—a gesture that made Sumin sadder than she'd been all day.

No rest, even with the child next to me.

Now was the time to go to the studio. Evening had not yet given way to night. It was light that gave you the illusion you could see more clearly than you could.

One of the cats was on the flagstones, watching something. Below her paw, a lizard appeared as though she'd invented it. Bending over to examine it had been more work for me than it should've been, and I rested for a moment with my hand on the latch before opening the door.

The cleaning woman had done a good job. I could smell her oil on the cherry bookcases and the armchair in the corner and something else, unidentifiable. My heart was beating hard. I couldn't see anything.

I closed my eyes to get my bearings.

There were smells missing: turpentine, developer.

I heard a small cough. And I identified the smell: the idiot reporter's aftershave. I opened my eyes. A shape took form across the room in the armchair.

"Um," he said.

I turned on a light.

"I hope you don't mind," he said.

"Of course I mind," I said.

He began his apologies, though not as wholeheartedly as he might've.

I waved my hand. "No, no," I said. "Don't make your position worse." Even with the light, I was having trouble focusing.

"Are you alright?" he asked, his tone less concerned than it should have been.

I didn't answer. I stood there conjuring details to quiet my heart.

The sound of the neighboring cows making their way to the barn. By the wicker chair, narcissus and mimosas. The Böcklin quote taped to the window. My own, pinned to the curtains bordering the developing tables: *The thinnest of lines where matter ends and mind begins.* And: *There are the things that I see. They are what is important. They are what we should preserve.*

He said he imagined that coming back here stirred up quite a few feelings. His voice was filled with delicacy. I found his assumptions despicable. Had I really expected more from the mooncalf my daughter had chosen?

I walked to the other armchair and sat down. I suggested he do less imagining and more observing. With the latter he might convince people that he was smarter than he was.

He said nothing, and the warmth of having put someone in their place melted through me.

"Should I go?" he asked.

"Don't be a child," I said.

He held up a framed photograph on the table by his chair. "Why leave this here?" he asked. "It's your family, isn't it?"

That last summer, after *Twelve*, I'd taken most of the books and personal items and left everything else. The developing equipment, the furniture, my own prints. I hadn't known I wouldn't work again. That had come upon me slowly, like somebody else's decision. Sometimes I still tried to blame Cam, but I knew she was not to blame. I knew her growing up may have been the reason the photographs of her had to stop, but it had nothing to do with why all image-making stopped. That I had to bear full responsibility for. Something had left me. I had needed her.

Grady repeated his question. His tone was aggressively casual. The photograph had been taken after our first dinner in Paris. My mother, father, myself and my new French family had trooped into another room where my new grandfather had arranged for a photograph. We had stood in two semicircular rows.

He held it out to me. I made no move to take it.

He pointed to the woman in the back center. "This is?" he prompted.

My father's mother, I told him.

His finger moved to the man on her right. "And this is your grandfather." His finger moved again. "And your father." He looked at me. "Is this difficult for you?" he asked.

I told him not to be ridiculous. I identified the others. In the front, my father's three sisters; on my new grandmother's left, myself, standing on a footstool, and then my mother.

I remembered the velvet hood, and the whirr of the shutter release. Grady waited. I said, "I remember it felt wonderful to be taller than my mother."

He returned to the photo. "What was she like? Your mother."

129

Again, that neutral tone. Hsing Chiang's face in the back of the plane. Alice's black hair against my white sheets. The week seemed dangerous in a palpable and imprecise way.

I went on slowly, examining my words for possible hidden meanings as they came out. I told him about the house in the French Concession of Shanghai. Two stones, enormous, in front of the entrance, polished blue with sitting. In the evenings, I sat there with Father, eating peanuts, watching our European neighbors come out of their houses to fan themselves on their doorsteps.

Mother, as always, stayed hidden. Chinese and wrong even in her own country.

In Paris, I was a half-caste, mixed blood, *yang kueitse*—devil from over the ocean. By 1937, it was clear that I would be safer in the States. Had my mother and father's safety even been discussed? Not that I could remember; not with me.

All that warring blood in Cam—Chinese, French, Japanese from the boy-father who left Sumin the instant he heard about the baby. And yet, she had the poise of someone who expected the world to give what it could, for the smallest price.

Grady interrupted to say that he had always felt Cam wasn't nearly as poised, as fearless as Sumin and I thought she was.

It was as if he had reached over and pressed a bruise on my thigh. I distracted myself by thinking of what unadulterated Alice might be capable of.

I asked if he knew the Chinese metaphor for integrity. "A well-formed bamboo in the chest." I made a fist and rapped myself on the chest. My mother had that.

I tried to clarify. My mother was a black face: in Chinese opera, a black face indicated courage.

He seemed uninterested in my culture lessons. He put the photo down and sat in the rocking chair opposite me. "I read somewhere that the photo *Bound Feet* was inspired by her," he said.

I'd told the story many times. The anxiety was dissolving.

I told him that a whole series of photos had been inspired, at least in part, by visual memory: watching my mother unwrap her feet at the end of the day. The basin of warm water I'd set beside her. I'd watch her unwrap and unwrap those long strips of cotton, sure that beneath the next layer had to be her feet.

He was silent. I found it disquieting. I'd come to expect small murmurs at this point, little noises of sympathy.

I went on: when I finally could see her feet, I could do nothing but stare at their astonishing grotesquerie.

"Mmm," he said.

It was a small noise, and there was something distracted about it.

When a bride was carried in the bridal chair to her husband's home, her shoes were the only part of her visible. The men along the way took subtle peeks, registering the tininess of the foot.

This way they knew how much jealousy to expend on the husband-to-be.

"What did your father think of your mother's tiny feet?" Grady asked.

"A good question," I said. "When we moved to Paris, she wanted to be like other women. She took off the binding cloths, wanting her feet to look normal, but of course, they could not. They'd been bound from age two, for several years. Years of wrapping the foot to break the toes, fold them under the sole.

"This could not be erased by undoing some bandages. The feet remained crippled and shrunken. She wore European shoes anyway. She stuffed them with cotton wool to fill the space."

I told him I escaped only because Father thought the whole idea barbaric. My father's goodness swam around me like a rebuke. I shook my head briskly.

I usually concluded with a final bit to bring the personal into the realm of the universal. What certain cultures required women to go through in the name of beauty was, of course, what many of the Cam photos attempted to address.

What more could he ask? I'd provided the segue into the work. He didn't seem to be listening.

"And because he was protecting you," he said.

It took me a minute to piece together what he was referring to. And even then I had the disturbing sense that I hadn't fully figured it out. I didn't say anything.

"Your mother," he finally said, "must've had a very difficult time once she moved back to China in 'sixty-two."

It was a statement. Heat went through me. I had the sensation he was waiting for information he already knew. How much could Hsing Chiang have known? Who else might he have spoken with?

I stood. I said, "She had a difficult time wherever she went. In China, she was a Chinese married to a foreigner against her family's wishes. In France, she was a Chinese amongst Europeans. After my father's death, the servants whispered fabrications about her. Oversights began to be made. Family would forget to tell her about visitors or engagements. Topics that she knew nothing about surfaced at the dinner table. Finally, she arranged to go back to China. In China in the sixties she was a woman who'd chosen to move away."

Grady waited, silent.

In old China, I told him, a woman who'd lost her husband had lost her identity. In new China, it was supposed to be different, but of course it wasn't. My mother had been the subject of ridicule and gossip by women embarrassed by the sight of a woman trying to stand on her own.

Grady said, "And China in the sixties was a particularly bad time to have foreign connections."

I congratulated him on his command of Chinese history.

"Not just her husband and her years in

France," he went on. "Most of all—it would seem to me—" He looked up, the modest reporter speculating. "You."

I said nothing.

"Your existence must've been..." Here he searched for just the right words. "Problematic."

"Well put," I said. I walked to the door and opened it. Something moved along the side of the studio. The sound of cicadas filled the room. "When you've had a life like mine," I said, "most aspects of it are."

"I would imagine," he said. "That you had somewhat of a choice."

I wanted this conversation to end. I thought of slipping into bed next to the child and laying her hand across my brow.

He gestured with his hand. "I mean in terms of how much, how much more, a part of that problem you would be."

He wasn't looking at me, but his antennae were out.

I held a warning finger up. "Don't think you understand everything because you've done a little homework."

The blue of late evening had ceded to surprisingly illuminating stars. I stepped outside; he followed, and I closed the door behind us. "I've always loved this time of day," I said, concentrating on taking slow, even breaths. "The time when simple games become less playful than malevolent."

Again, Grady seemed not to be listening. "It's much like the choice facing you now," he added. "In terms of what to do about Alice."

"I don't think so," I said.

The sound from the side of the studio repeated itself and Alice appeared out of the darkness, the white of her nightgown standing out above all else, a dress on a hanger.

She was wide awake. "Why are you talking about me?" she said.

I stepped towards her and reached for where I thought her hand might be. "I'm not," I said.

"I heard you," she said. "When I'm asleep," she said, "you shouldn't talk about me."

Grady stood like a cow.

"I'm not talking about you," I repeated. "Grady is."

She looked at him.

"Say goodnight to Grady," I said.

And she did, and we made our way back to the house, my hand on her shoulder, her fingers gripping the corner of my nightgown—an odd and unlikely *pas de deux*.

~~~

*A*fter dinner, Grady had disappeared and Sumin sat there watching her daughter until Cam made a face and said, "Stop staring." And when Sumin couldn't, Cam groaned and stomped over to the stereo.

The music seemed to cheer them up. Cam examined the CD cover and moved her hips to the music.

"What is this?" Sumin asked.

It turned out to be something called the Fine Young Cannibals. Cam held the cover up for her mother to see. It featured an exotic-looking man's face.

"Another half-breed," Cam said, pointing at it.

They both looked at the cover for a while.

"You might lose her," Sumin finally said.

Cam put the CD down. "I know," she said. She wasn't angry.

Sumin peered at her. She still couldn't figure out the nature of her daughter's scars.

Cam was singing along.

Sumin watched her dance. She wanted those scars to be there; she wanted to be responsible for them, as if she herself had made the cut and then sewed up the wound.

⟡

Tonight the things I counted on were no longer rock-solid. The tension between the terror and the seductiveness of the terror kept me awake throughout the night, bats and fireflies my company.

I outlasted the falling of late night, layer by layer. I outlasted Alice's questions.

I outlasted the moon. Two more hours would color the windows blue. And I would not sleep, the camera standing in the room beneath mine.

My last visit before she died, I woke to find my mother sitting on my windowsill watching me sleep. Her silhouette diffused as the sky behind her lightened.

The 1937 International Exhibition. The

German pavilion on one side of the Champs de Mars; the Soviet on the other. My father glumly referred to them as the image of the future. I was too captivated by what the hundreds of commissioned artists had done with light. The Eiffel Tower wore eight kilometers of fluorescent tubes. The light beams between the pavilions were awesome exchanges of fire.

Many displays of France's colonies. A reconstruction of the Temple of Angkor Wat. My mother looked as if she worked there.

My father could not tear himself away from Picasso's *Guernica*, then the timely thing. I was more interested in Calder's *Mercury Fountain*, in front of it: a round pool of mercury with what looked like a giant iron grasshopper drinking from it. I liked throwing coins in and watching them float.

I observed Alice. Each limb flung in a different direction. A war victim.

What did I want? I wanted her.

Tuesday

Sumin woke early again and went to listen outside the living-room door. Grady had suggested he sleep in the living room. That was where his stuff was: papers, notes, and laptop. He reminded her that they'd said they would try to make the interview as normal as possible. She had asked if this was about the interview or about their "wait and see" stage. He had looked pained and shrugged. She'd felt bad and had ended up telling him to sleep where he wanted in a brisker way than she'd intended. Mostly, she'd been worried about Cam's reaction to the separate beds. So far, her daughter hadn't had one.

She heard his snoring and she settled on the porch in that same chair, this time with a book. The book had a middle-aged woman protagonist who was forever looking back over her life and seeing things clearly for the first time. The woman ran into a former husband, visited an old school, returned to her childhood home to care for her ailing parents, and after a prophylactic fling with a guy who was supposed to be dreamy but turned out to be only oily, she came out of things better and smarter.

Later, washing yet more dishes—had everyone gotten up for a midnight snack?—she considered that at least the protagonist was the center of things. She wasn't the center of anything.

No one seemed interested in breakfast. Alice wanted to call her mother again. "It's at night there," she said. "I counted."

Cam looked at Celine. Celine dialed the numbers, and all of them stood around watching Alice listen to the ringing on the other end.

Celine announced that she and Cam were going to take Alice on a tour.

"Sshh," Alice said.

Finally Celine took the receiver from Alice's hand and replaced it in the cradle. They could call again when they got back. Grady cleared his throat, reminded everyone about his interview and suggested that the tour might include both himself and some of the old shoot sites. Alice wrinkled her nose. "Not more photographs," she said. What Sumin was going to do was apparently not an issue.

To balance things out, Sumin insisted that *she* be the one to take Alice upstairs to get ready.

Alice wanted to know: What were they going to see? Was there anything good in the woods? What kind of animals? How long did it take to get there? Would she have to walk the whole way? What were they going to see? Could she call her mother when she got back?

Sumin sat her on the bed to tie her shoes. "So," she said. "How often do you call your mother anyway?"

Alice said she didn't know.

Sumin tried to tie the laces while Alice's feet swung back and forth. "And are you guys going to visit each other or..." Sumin trailed off.

Alice asked when she could call again.

"Right when you get back from your adventure," Sumin said.

"It's not an adventure," Alice said. "I need bug stuff." She held out her arms.

Sumin located the bug spray. Alice stood up and closed her eyes tight.

"What does your mother say?" Sumin asked.

"I don't know," Alice said.

Sumin rubbed repellent onto her legs. "Does Cam tell you how long she thinks you'll live with her?"

"I don't know," Alice said. "Get the back of my neck."

She bent her head down, flipping her hair out of the way, and Sumin stared at her tiny neck.

"If you could choose, where would you want to live?" she asked.

Alice looked up, considering. "I want," she said absentmindedly, as if she'd already forgotten the question. She looked at Sumin. "I don't want to tell you," she said. She pulled her socks up higher and ran downstairs.

From the kitchen window, Sumin watched the expedition cross the back meadow. When they were out of sight she scrubbed the last dish so vigorously that the finish around the plate's edge started to flake off. While she did this she summoned up her determination to talk with Celine about the interview idea, but each time she tried to imagine how the conversation would go, she found herself bothered by two other topics: Grady's interest in her grandmother, and Alice. They seemed connected in ways she felt unqualified to figure out. She could just hear her mother's reactions to such intuitions.

To make herself feel better, she arranged the pantry cupboard and the refrigerator. At home she had clear plastic containers holding raw cashews, crackers, rice, cereal, whatever, arranged in size order in rows. She kept her candy in glass jars in the crisper.

Here she did what she could. She poured the milk out of the cardboard carton into a glass pitcher. She put the coffee beans in an old peanut-butter jar in the freezer. She ran out of containers before the cereal, but put the boxes in size order, anyway.

That took a half hour. She stood with her hands on her hips in the center of the kitchen. Outside, big clouds were blowing by fast. The kitchen went from light to dark and back again. She did not feel better.

She thought about reading. She had another book with another middle-aged woman protagonist. She thought about writing in her journal. Instead, she decided to poke through Grady's notes. It was just the kind of aggression she was good at: the kind that no one would know about, the kind with no consequences.

———

A BED OF pine needles. A small girl lying across them on her belly, her face turned to the camera. At intervals across her bare back, moxibustion cups, five total. The girl's skin suctions up into the squat glass cups. The tiny cones of moxa burn, filling the glass with a light grey smoke.

Light through overhead trees spots her back. Her legs are cut off at mid-thigh.

Adult female hands reach into the frame to apply the sixth cup. The photo is called Asthma.

❧

*W*ind. Fan-shaped clouds.

We walked to the far end of the back meadow. Just inside a stand of evergreens there was a small clearing with a circle of pine stumps like an arranged meeting ground. Our own little Stonehenge.

Cam called for us to look. She and Alice were back-to-back on a stump. Their arms were linked, and Cam was bending forward as far as she could. Alice lay backwards across Cam's arched back, her feet dangling. It was a version of one of the first photos we'd used the summer she was six. The sunlight through the trees bisected the two girls. Alice was smiling and the white line of her teeth shone.

Grady was considering them. "They're more like sisters than mother and daughter, aren't they?" he said.

Last night's conversation hung between us.

The landscape and Cam, I told him, were both slow to give up secrets, always out there, underfoot, seemingly so accessible.

"Seemingly?" he asked, still watching.

An open smile and closed soul. Like I taught her, I said.

Cam scoffed. She stood up, placing Alice beside her on the stump, then pirouetted in place, twisting her legs, then her arms, and finally her wrists and hands. The trees swayed above her. She was entwined with light. Alice pushed her off the stump, then jumped off herself.

Cam looked at us. "Aren't you guys supposed to be talking?" she asked.

Grady laughed. It took me by surprise, and I realized that he hadn't done so much at all since his arrival. I was surprised, too, at how appealing his laughter was. The depth of it, the genuine pleasure it expressed. The elegant lines of his smile. He was not, I realized, an unattractive man. Less American than European-looking. The kind of man who seemed perfectly suited for brown suede.

"Was she a pliant model?" he asked.

I nodded, beginning to walk the path to the pond. "In the sense that she cooperated."

He followed me. "What other sense is there?" he asked. I let it go, a foolish question.

Our steps made little sound against the pine needles. I inhaled. Cam rushed by like a dog who needed to be first. Her smell mixed with

144

pine and sun. Alice lagged behind, stopping every so often to pick up things, then throw them down again. She found a stick and struck trees.

I spoke without turning. "Our shoots were magical usually when the weather was strange— cold or uncommonly foggy. Hours together with both of us barely breathing. The mist shut in our sounds and the sounds of the woods and turned everything into a conspiracy. In the quiet, the click of the camera. The rustle of Cam adjusting position. I gave instructions with my hand so as not to disturb the calm."

I amused myself at how much I was sharing, given last night. We emerged onto the edge of the pond. Grady, of course, did not ask the logical follow-up question: Which photos had come out of such shoots?

Cam immediately colonized the end of the little dock, and stirred the water with her toes. Grady and I stayed in the shadow of the woods, watching. Alice passed us and stepped warily onto the dock.

Grady said, "She looks as if she thinks it might collapse at any moment."

"Ssh," I said, watching.

The trick had always been to await the moment when everything was in balance.

When Alice reached her, Cam held the girl's hand while she lowered herself carefully to the edge of the dock. Cam bent to take off the girl's shoes and socks. Banal movements were filled with extraordinary tenderness. Even sitting, Alice balanced herself with a hand on Cam's shoulder.

Every time I developed, I was wrought up, believing I'd nearly gotten what I was after, but had failed. What must the frustrated experimenting of the early masters have been like? Poor Wedgwood, soaking white paper and white leather in silver-nitrate solution, unable to figure out a way to desensitize the paper once the image was fixed.

He'd been forced to show them only furtively, in his darkroom, by the light of a candle.

Nine times out of ten for me as well, failure.

But every tenth attempt: everyone, having looked, would not only see, but hear. When Cam opened her eyes a certain way and turned them on the lens, it was as if a high note on a Bösendorfer had been struck.

My eyes roved from the backs of their heads to the far edge of the pond. Cattails. A bullfrog sounding somewhere deep within. That serenity had been almost completely elusive since the photos had stopped. I glanced back at Alice. It was only one of the reasons I was drawn to her.

"This place means a great deal to you," Grady finally said.

What powers of observation, I thought. But his tone was subdued, almost sad. I rested my hand on his forearm and pointed. A blue heron was delicately picking its way across the far bank. I took my hand back. Even during the hard parts of the summers, I told him—Sumin's resentments, Cam's colds—all this and I were great friends.

I wasn't so much lying as recreating the

truth. This place too had just been part of a constant, unfulfilled search. Even before the Cam photographs began, everyone who knew me at all would have said that this place—its balance, its sense of serene order—was what I was searching for. I encouraged such notions.

The heron took off, skimming the bulrushes, and disappeared around the tip of the far woods.

Cam stretched. Her arms made a Y in the air.

"I'm bored," I heard Alice say.

Cam said something in response.

"Cam is like a water lily," I said. I told him about the species of daylily used as a charm for dispelling grief. Women wore it in their girdles to increase their chances for conceiving sons.

"Was Sumin as beautiful at the same age?" Grady asked.

I started for the dock. "No," I said.

Cam looked up when I reached her. I stood next to her and palmed the back of her head. I didn't like her new haircut. Weaving my fingers through it, I said, "You are a golden phoenix amongst us chickens."

Cam stood up beside me. "Snore," she said. She walked back up the dock and linked arms with Grady. "Don't print this stuff."

Alice tapped my shin. "Where are the tractors?" she asked.

A friend once asked, half-joking, "Why photograph Cam? She's already beautiful."

How much of an impetus had envy been for

me? A girl in my Shanghai school: I'd been as striking as she, but she was full Chinese, the crane amongst the chickens. Cam, even Sumin, had always looked more authentic than I.

Cam led Grady further around the pond. "Come on," she said. "You can interview *me*."

Alice let out a squawk. We all stared. "No more talking," she said.

"Horses," she said, pointing vehemently. "Tractors," she said, pointing to another spot.

We tried various things. Cam was inept at dealing with her. Grady stooped and reminded her that it was his job to talk to people. She considered him. "Nobody likes you," she said.

Cam took him by the arm. "Come on," she said. "We're going on. She can stay here."

A mothering technique undoubtedly learned from Sumin.

He was reluctant, but allowed himself to be led away. I stayed and asked her why she was so mad.

She wouldn't answer, and after a minute, I followed the others.

Up ahead, Grady was laughing. I couldn't hear what they were saying.

Dragons bear dragons, phoenixes bear phoenixes, and moles bear sons accomplished in digging holes. My mother: what her existence in my blood meant for me. Sumin, and her endless stream of failures.

During our first months in Paris, family

friends came by in droves. Ostensibly out of respect but mostly out of curiosity. They fingered my mother's silks. They eyed her jade with envy, and me with something similar, as if I were an enigmatic object pulled from the folds of my mother's gown. Alice must feel some of this.

I could hear her behind me. I didn't turn around. Children benefit from being left alone.

Grady and Cam were pulling farther ahead, towards the honeysuckle caves. Their speed made me walk slower. When they looked back I waved them on.

The children of my father's friends had become my new playmates. They'd felt that the rules of European privacy did not apply to me. I found them in my drawers, across my bed, wearing my shoes. They broke my ink sticks to see what was inside. I snatched the pieces from one boy's hands, yelling, "Get out, get out. Out of my room, you rat-faced white." He'd stared at me, and I at him, wishing that my accent was better, wishing for a more satisfying outlet for my rage.

Behind me, Alice muttered about "some people."

Those early years in Paris, I'd continually come up against the walls of my own limitations. Mother, too, had cried and cried. One of our solaces had been my hair. In China, she'd combed it each night and morning—one hundred strokes. We'd giggled about the old saying: "Women have long hair and short intelligence."

149

In Paris, she continued to spend hours on it. The servants were forbidden to touch it. I sat in front of her on my bed, letting her style until her quiet sobs eased to a halt, and I could turn and take the brush from her hand and sit with her, covering her hands with mine.

It hadn't taken long to realize that the way to survive was to divorce myself from those cries, become European in ways she never could. It was necessary no matter what the consequences for her. And so when I was fifteen or sixteen I used my savings and went with a French friend to the famous Antoine's salon to have my hair cut and permed. My mother was so distraught afterwards that even my father tried to talk to me.

He had spoken to me the same way after the war about coming home to visit. I did, twice, but by 1947, my landscapes were selling well. I couldn't leave now, I told him. Perhaps next year. No, a visit from them wouldn't work either. My mother never asked for visits directly, but I knew his anger was on her behalf. In his final letter, he wrote that he would not contact me again. Almost immediately after his death, I began showing regularly in Paris. I took trip after trip, contacting my mother on every second or third one.

When my mother moved back to China and the old sayings about dragons, phoenixes and moles began to surface again in the pronouncements of the new government, I knew that it was not good news for her. She was the daughter of wealthy merchant parents. Her husband was a Frenchman. She'd chosen to leave China for France. No matter that she'd also chosen to go back. I was proof of her connections to the corrupt West. I made reactionary art. I knew she'd suffer as a result of my existence. The only question was how much. Grady's comment from last night returned. How much could he know? What was he planning on doing with his information?

I couldn't walk any farther. I steadied myself against a tree. It seemed hotter. My pulse again. I mouthed the words I used in interviews when inept reporters would ask about the exploitive aspect of my work: Love is not a feeling. Love is seeing. Love is not a feeling. Love is seeing. I stood there, mouthing to myself what I used to mouth to others.

UNTITLED

FROM LEFT TO right: Part of a tree trunk. Thick, substantial, tapering towards the top of the frame. Chips, whorls and grooves play across it. Around its girth, a rope, dark against the tree's light bark.

Next, from behind the tree, the back of a teenaged girl. Her bare shoulder, the back and side of her baseball cap. One ear.

Finally, another girl, from the back, her wrists tied behind her and to the tree. She is naked and she looks over her shoulder, past the first girl, past

the tree, almost to the camera. The rope goes
around her wrists and forearms in Xs, like the straps
on roman sandals. Her flesh bulges around it. Her
arms are pulled up behind her. Her elbows jut out.
Beneath the rope, her lower back, her bottom, her
thighs. Above them, the wave of her spine, her
twisted neck, the side of her face.

~&~

othing in the notes struck Sumin as very
surprising.

"Her work witnesses a world it seems urgent to
remember."

The recognition of a rhythm in the world of real
things.

The contradictions in the hidden, with light that
quietly eats around and into a thing.

Most of them she remembered from various
reviews and catalog prefaces. Her aggressive
act started to seem less aggressive. This
depressed her more. She sat in the rocking chair
and thought of those four off on their tour. The
breeze coming through the room was unusually cool. Goose bumps appeared on her arms,
and she rubbed them, going back to her
reading.

The accordian folder on the Cultural Revolution was a surprise.

The details of Red Guard torture tech-
niques were a surprise.

The news that Celine's mother had died in
September 1967 was not a surprise, but that
it had been a suicide: that was a surprise.

Late June in Beijing: the pale heat. The parks filled with the odor of insecticides.

I was really not feeling well. I made it to the bench made of hewn logs just off the path. My back between my shoulder blades ached from the strain of breathing.

Alice sat next to me. "What are you doing?" she asked.

"Sitting," I said. "And thinking."

"Why are you sitting?" she asked.

"To think," I said.

She poked a leaf through the bench slats. I tried to make my breathing quieter.

Winter visits to Mother's new Beijing home. Her coal burners centered in every room. The blue rumors of flame within the coal cylinders and the expertise necessary to keep them burning. Adding a new cylinder meant trying to match the holes just so. The heat reached only a short distance into the room. They smelled.

"I'm thinking about horses and tractors," she said.

I nodded. "I'm thinking about my mother," I said.

"Me, too," she said, then fell silent, her hands folded in her lap.

Once she moved back to China, my mother had made direct and repeated attempts to persuade me and Sumin to come and live with her. It wasn't right, she said, that she had to be alone in her old age. I could see how much it humiliated her to have to ask. Neither of us could hear her pleas without hearing my father's earlier appeals on her behalf. My refusals were echoes.

She bought me gifts: furniture, books, paintings. She bought a battery-operated heater, installed picture windows. You could work here, she said. In peace.

I was dizzy. I touched Alice's head. She didn't react. "You want very much to go live with your mother, don't you?" I asked.

She shook her head. "I don't want to go there," she said. "I want her to come back here."

Of course, I thought. What could I give her? What could I install that would make her want me—the old woman?

I considered her. When it was her turn for betrayal, what would she do? Would she cut and perm her hair?

"Come," I said, pulling her onto the ground. "I'll show you something."

We knelt next to each other, and I cleared a space in front of us of pine needles, leaves and twigs. My hands left fan-shaped track marks in the red dirt.

"What are we doing?" she said, always skeptical.

I gave her a stick and showed her how to hold it, then covered her hand with mine. She smelled of suntan lotion and bug spray, and beneath that, of melon.

And we wrote. Character after character, erasing each before even discussing what it had meant. I learned how to write with the whole arm, from the shoulder, how to see the entire ideogram before filling the square on the practice paper, how to imagine the square when it was no longer there.

Calligraphy made me see that every object was an ideogram. The beginning of seeing in pictures. And black and white.

Meiyoubanfa: Nothing can be done. We wrote the phrase several times, until Alice pulled her hand away from mine and said, "Okay, okay. I'll do it myself."

I lifted myself back up to the bench, still feeling dizzy, my eyesight in and out of focus. She erased all but one of our sentences, and sat with one knee up, one leg tucked underneath her, to copy it. I watched.

Before the Cam photos, I might have considered my mother's request. In 1962 I was idle and at a loss, still feeling the after-effects of the blacklisting. Still using it as the excuse for the lack of new work. But after Cam was born, there was no question. After the first Cam book, all those who had ignored me had come around. In China, *drawing* the naked body was considered revisionist—a "yellow work of art." Again, I chose art over family. I turned away from my mother in order to face Cam.

It is not the Chinese way to be involved in other people's troubles.

Love is seeing, I thought. It is, and I didn't. "*Meiyoubanfa,*" I said out loud.

Alice kept writing. "Stop talking to yourself," she said.

I mouthed the words instead.

155

Cam was behind me. She put her hands on my shoulders. "Celine," she said, "are you okay?"

Alice looked up. "She's talking to herself," she said.

Cam's new haircut was my mother's. The one forced on her when she moved back to China. All her beautiful hair cut bluntly to her ear.

"Celine?" she said again.

Grady was behind her. I erased the characters with my foot. I couldn't tell whether he'd seen anything. Cam, of course, didn't speak or read Chinese.

"Hey," Alice protested.

"Feeling better?" Cam asked.

Alice looked at her like she had no idea what she was talking about.

"What're you working on?" Grady asked.

Alice stood up and brushed herself off. "We're writing."

"Oh," Grady said, staring at the dirt.

"*Meiyoubanfa,*" Alice said, her accent unaffected by five years in the States.

Grady raised his eyebrows. "That's an interesting practice phrase," he said.

He respected my silence for a moment. Then he said he wanted to know about two photos: *Monsters on Parade* and *Snake Spirits.*

I felt a visceral wariness. But he was no mind reader.

"I always thought those were lame," Cam said. "I had to be the vehicle of Celine's guilt over the Cultural Revolution."

Alice took three or four exaggerated steps, dragging her toes in the dirt. She said she was going to find Sumin. Maybe *she* would take her to the tractors.

Cam told her she couldn't go back alone. Alice said she could. I told Cam to let her go. And she did. We watched her small shape make its way down the path, and then Grady returned to his inquisition.

"Guilt about what?" he asked.

They joined me on the bench. A rodent of some sort tried to negotiate an elm root across the trail and slipped.

"That *Monsters* one, I had to walk around in circles wearing a wooden sign for hours," Cam said.

Our bench had a view of the house. I watched for Alice. Cam, always restless, sat cross-legged on the ground in front of us. She looked up at Grady. "It was heavy."

"I'm sorry," he said. "I wasn't sufficiently sympathetic."

Even Cam had to smile.

I said, "Portrait sitters in 1840 had to sit for eight to ten minutes, in intense sunlight, while the artist promenaded around them, watch in hand, calling out the time every five seconds."

Neither responded.

"Is anyone going to tell me about those pictures?" he asked.

Cam said, "She got some neighbor kids to be the Red Guards. They got to carry bamboo spears with red tassels."

Grady was looking at her, but his focus was me.

"I," Cam said, "got to wear the dunce cap and the badge of shame. The *heavy* badge of shame."

She looked at me. I said, "The other children were delighted with Cam as the victim. She was the object of much of their envy."

"How lucky you were there to facilitate that," Grady said.

Cam looked suddenly focused. "That isn't true," she said. She was staring at her hands in her lap. "That's just what I convinced myself of." She seemed to be talking to herself.

I was silent.

Cam exhaled and stretched out across the trail and closed her eyes. Her face made small movements, seeking out the sun.

The same sun baked the back of my neck. I was tired, still light-headed. I couldn't last here much longer.

"Why *Snake Spirits*?" Grady asked. "As a title?"

Cam said, "Cow ghosts and snake spirits. The reactionaries during the Cultural Revolution."

Grady wanted my answer. So I explained: supernatural creatures from mythology who had the ability to disguise themselves as human. Once recognized for what they were, their power was extinguished.

Again I had the disturbing sensation that I was telling him things he knew. I reviewed my words. My hands were needled with heat.

Have you truly come to the point in your life when you can be outmanuevered by him? I thought. And then I entertained a more chilling thought concerning the consequences of being outmanuevered.

I stood up and offered my hand to Cam. "Come," I said. "Let's go in."

❧

UNTITLED

AN ARMCHAIR IN the middle of a field. On it, a faded print of a child wrapped in padded silk. On her head, a tiny fur hat. China, late nineteenth century. She stares straight at the camera.

To the right of the print and the chair, the body of a girl in a bikini from breast to knee. Her arm is draped over the back of the chair. Her legs are spotted with insect bites. Her belly swells slightly. The one breast you can see is sprinkled with water, and the damp spot from her hand spreads across the top of the chair. There are no shadows.

❧

A single small sheet of paper with shaky characters in ballpoint pen running down the center. Grady had covered it in clear plastic. A translation was paper-clipped to the back:

I am the common enemy of the people. In order not to poison others surrounding me, I am

*determined to be liquidated from society. Long
live the Great Proletarian Revolution!*

*To my daughter, Li Na: I have shamed you.
Any troubles you have had, I am the cause.*

Long Live Chairman Mao!

Huying

Sumin sat on the floor with the folder.
Where had Grady gotten this? How is it that
she hadn't known about it? She racked her
memory concerning Celine's trip to her
mother's funeral. It had been 1967, within a
month of *One*'s publication. Celine hadn't
wanted Sumin and Cam along. Cam had been
only two and Celine had said the trip was
too long and too dangerous.

Celine had gone. Celine had come back.

The second page in the folder, in Grady's
handwriting: *Steel wire tightened with pliers. Wrists
white. Maggots.*

*In the North: the accused forced to kneel on
broken glass and rock. To crawl around and eat
grass. Knives in chairseats. Baths in boiling
water. The "yin-yang haircut": one side shaved.*

The photo from *Six*: Cam, in partial darkness, holding scissors above the newly shaved
side of her mother's head. Celine had insisted
that it be done to Sumin—it wasn't the same
if it was a stranger.

Sumin hadn't been asked to participate all
that often.

*A dulian—three-line poem posted around doors.
Vertical lines comprise antithetical couplet, the
horizontal line summarizes. Summer of 1966, on*

a door in Beijing: "The old man a true man, the son is a hero. The old man a reactionary, the son is an asshole. It is basically so."

The Red Guard anthem:
The old man a true man, the son is a hero,
The old man a reactionary, the son is an
*   asshole.*
If you are revolutionary, then step forward
*   and come along,*
If you are not, damn you to hell.

Be faithful to the revolution and the
*   party,*
The party is our mother and father.
Whoever dares say one bad word about the
*   party,*
We'll send him to Yama immediately.

Damn you to hell!
Depose you from your fucking post!
Kill! Kill! Kill!

It all made Sumin feel like what she was—a stranger coming across someone else's research. She had to keep reminding herself that these were her grandmother and her mother.

She glanced at her watch.

The next page was typed: *"Sweep Away All Monsters"—editorial urging the purge of bourgeois ideology, June 1, 1966.*

1966—Intellectuals (millions) sent to rural labor camps. "Going to the Countryside," train stations filled with people seeing everybody off with drums and gongs. Ways of getting back: manufactured illnesses—swallowed nails or coins. Cut hands, blood in stools.

Five Black categories: landlords, rich peasants, counterrevolutionaries, Rightists and "bad elements."

Struggle Sessions—meetings held in public to denounce. Immediate physical punishment and humiliation.

Next to this note, in the margin, Grady's handwriting: *Huying—150? 175?* Sumin couldn't make sense of these notes. Farther down the margin, in tiny letters: *dunce cap made from wastepaper basket and paper? Forced to stand on chair, turn around in tight circles.*

Cam had worn a little circular path in the tall grass during the shooting of *Monsters on Parade.*

Beatings in the evenings, not on faces. Shut in cowshed, forced to slap each other. Ears deformed by pliers.

Sumin's knees were sore. She rocked back on the balls of her feet, playing a little balancing game.

She had to get out of his room. It was late afternoon. She picked out pages she thought might contain the most useful information, folded them once and tucked them into the waistband of her pants. She pulled her shirt down over them and checked to see if they were noticeable.

She replaced what she'd already read, including the plastic-covered suicide note.

She stood up and put the accordian folder

back on the table. The pages under her shirt were tickling. She rearranged them.

To my daughter, Li Na: I have shamed you. Any troubles you have had, I am the cause.

She was crying.

She pressed her hands against her eyes. She was crying for herself. Some of the tenets of the Cultural Revolution were Celine's own philosophy: No speaking out or acting on your own ideas. You are not to feel as if you've been wronged.

She was crying because her mother had never said anything like the contents of this note to her, and reading the note made her want that more than anything. There she stood, slobbering herself with tears and thinking the discovery of this note made no difference; there was nothing she could do to get out of her life.

This was how Alice found her. And to Sumin's surprise, Alice didn't ask anything. Just came up next to her and rested her head on Sumin's belly, as if she'd been coming across crying women all day.

Alice stood there, and Sumin's tears gave way to the sense that there were connections between Alice and the note, and all Sumin had to do was figure out what they were and what they could mean for her life.

~

Cam wanted to stay, and Grady said he would stay with her. I hesitated, but then walked back alone. Only one memory on the way to the house. Of Sumin, surprisingly, at about ten, in autumn.

Walking in the woods, we came across the neighboring farmer chopping down a birch full of golden leaves. We walked closer. The farmer shouted and the tree tipped and fell at Sumin's feet. Right at her feet. The branches nearly engulfed her. They were her own borealis of color. It was an outstanding moment. One of the only times, maybe the only time, I remembered her as truly beautiful.

Wednesday

No sleep last night. More bothersome than the insomnia was the fact that Grady was its cause.

I surveyed the child, envying sleep. The last two nights, she'd had enormous trouble falling asleep, but once there, she'd been dead to the world.

How could Cam assert that she hadn't been envied? Had she really grown to believe that?

I pulled the sheet away. Her nightgown was twisted around her legs. I straightened her legs, then stretched her arms above her head. The clasping of the hands was her own contribution.

I sat on the bed and stroked the tops of her feet. Even relaxed, her toes bent back slightly, as if flexed. Her skin was so soft it made my own seem softer. She stirred and I stopped, still feeling her on my fingertips.

La règle guérit de tout. Discipline is the cure for everything. I stopped arguing with my body when the sky lightened and went downstairs and surveyed the new camera. It stood clean and unused. Sumin was coughing upstairs. Grady was moving around in the living room. My mother used to say that a young wife who had an old husband was another man's woman. I was too weary of the mess Sumin had made of her life to further inquire into the subject. I unscrewed the camera from the tripod, folded it as quietly as possible and put it in its bag. The bag over one shoulder, the tripod over the other, I headed outside.

The birds were asleep. The night's storm was represented by red softened ruts in the driveway, and at the door to my studio, some fragments of slate. Mornings in the Shanghai house smelled like wet earth. Through my bedroom window came the sounds of streetworkers throwing water to dampen the dusty streets.

The wet flagstone path approximated the jade called Light in Darkness from which chieftains had goblets made. It was said to change color in contact with poison.

The storm had beaten down the tall grass in the lower meadow. I made my way through it. The winds were gone. The heat was gathering like another storm. The air was damp. Moisture misted my upper lip and brow.

I missed being strong. I missed my strong shoulders.

I wanted to stop but the desire to get out of sight of the cabin was more persuasive. I must have looked ridiculous: a seventy-five-year-old woman stumbling across uneven ground with the tools of her former trade.

What was I doing? I hadn't set up a shot in years.

The signs in Shanghai parks read: No

DOGS. NO CHINESE. The first time I saw them, I wondered if I could pass for full French. I was tall for an eleven-year-old, and I had my father's narrow face and deep-set eyes. But then my mother's face had appeared in front of me. This from the daughter of the man who would spend the war quietly giving his seat on the Métro to strangers wearing the yellow star.

Two deer, suddenly alert to my presence, froze. I stopped and returned the attention.

On the path in the woods, I proceeded even more slowly. I strained my eyes to keep the path visible.

I came to the clearing with the circle of pine stumps, chose one, and sat, the tripod across my thighs. The camera I eased to the ground.

At twelve, Cameron wore boys' shirts over the breasts of a child bride. She swam underwater like a shark. Last year's swimsuit shoulder strap stretched and broke. Hems rose against the growth of twelve months.

People said about the photos that they never saw anything like that in their own children. I let it go. In such images, my life seemed thrown back at me in patterns and repetitions that I couldn't call my own. After the age of twelve, there is nothing of mystery. Nothing to spend one's time figuring out. Now, I looked at Cam and saw poise and authority, but no purity, no sense of the essential.

I found the tripod some footing amidst the

pine needles. I took the camera from its bag and stood, embarrassed by my own stiffness.

The sun was up now. The air a dusty yellow. The temperature had jumped ten degrees. September in Shanghai was "autumn tiger." Still air filled with the sound of a million locusts.

I reassembled the camera. I had trouble with the new, stiff movements of the lensboard. I attached the camera to the tripod. I inserted the film holder.

I tried to focus on an edge of light against the far curve of the stump, but the line wouldn't hold. My arm grew sore. I tried various grips on the focusing knob. I straightened up and pressed my fists into the small of my back.

I sat back down. A stump without Cam was just a stump. But I was picturing Alice, shadows netting her legs. Her posture on the dock. Her fingers dusted with dirt. And beneath every movement, frustration and anger and sadness.

I held my hands out in front of me. Was I speaking of subject or artist?

What had I been thinking, coming here?

A fabricated image of my mother's hands: the swelling from the handcuffs. The purple nails.

Officially, she hadn't been imprisoned; she'd "disappeared." Officially, she'd returned home after several months to jump into Superior Peace Lake. When I received the official death notice, I remembered the childhood superstition that dragons were in charge of water. It was important not to do anything to offend them.

❧

Cam had spent the previous afternoon and evening down by the pond sketching her own hands.

The next morning she asked Grady to model for her.

Grady said, yes, sure, with exactly that much fluster, glancing Sumin's way.

Cam sipped her tea standing by the sink, and closed her eyes lazily. "Good," she said. "Thanks." She pulled one foot up and rested it against her knee: the wading bird. Her nightshirt rode up her leg.

Some tea sloshed out of Sumin's mug.

"Tea water misbehaving?" Cam asked.

Grady laughed.

Sumin turned around and said, "Are you giggling? Is that a giggle?" She reached past him for a paper towel. "How old are you?"

The bitterness in her voice surprised her.

Cam raised her eyebrows. "If I were you," she said to Grady, "I'd steer clear."

He smiled.

Sumin faced the counter. "Alice not up yet?" she asked, unable to keep herself from pettiness.

"And where'd you guys sleep last night?" Cam returned, always willing to both rise to and derail her mother's challenges. She left the kitchen and climbed the stairs.

They waited for her noises to fade before turning to look at each other. Grady didn't look as embarrassed as he should. She washed Cam's mug and her own. She splashed water around the basin, turned off the tap and wiped the bowl and the rim of the sink dry with a paper towel. She swiped the length of the faucet twice, erasing the dry water marks. As a final touch, she pressed a towel-wrapped finger into its mouth. She didn't know why she did these kinds of things.

Grady watched the whole process.

She looked at him, finally, and he switched his mug to the hand farther from her. She didn't smile.

He asked if she'd seen any of his notes. He was missing some.

The pages were upstairs between her mattress and box spring. "I'm not allowed in there," she said. "We want to keep things as normal as possible."

He said quietly, "Circumstances haven't been normal for a few months now."

She looked at the floor. He was waiting.

Alice came downstairs in the middle of this, wanting her waffle. Her hair was a tornado and her eyes were puffy.

Sumin asked if she'd been crying.

"No," Alice responded.

Grady was still waiting. She wanted to say something that wouldn't cause him pain, and that might encourage him to help her use this new information. The only thing that occurred to her was one of his notes: *Jiang xin bi xin—imagine my heart is yours.* She couldn't offer this, so she offered nothing.

Alice sat at the table, waiting for her breakfast. She looked at Grady. "We were in your room yesterday," she said.

"Oh?" Grady said, keeping his tone neutral.

"Can I have extra syrup?" she asked Sumin.

Sumin had trouble with the frozen-waffle box.

Grady looked at her sadly. "Well," he said. "If you see them, let me know."

She wished he would both stay and go. "Okay," she said.

"Thanks," he said. He kept standing there.

She recalled a hug he had surprised her with a few weeks into their relationship. It had been so forceful, they had fallen backwards onto the couch, and even then he hadn't let go. It was like he had wanted his whole six-foot-four-inch body to fit inside of her. It was like he would never let go. His need, his happiness with her as the source, had thrilled her so exquisitely that she convinced herself what she was feeling was terror.

He turned to go and then turned back. "It's just that they don't make much sense in bits and pieces," he said.

She didn't know what to make of the comment or its tone. He left. She wouldn't let Alice have extra syrup. But then she asked if Alice wanted to take a walk down to the stables. Alice said she would like to, but later, and Sumin watched her eat and told her to let her know when she was ready.

171

It was cooler by the pond. I'd carried the tripod and camera until I couldn't manage anymore and had left them in the shade by a rock, deciding to get them on my way back to the house.

I spent time watching insects: ladybugs, water bugs, dragonflies. The latter hovered, cradling themselves.

Flying beetles sounded as they approached and receded like passing autos.

After she'd moved back to China, I spent long stretches of my visits to my mother picking caterpillars off the rain lilies in her front yard. By way of some bureaucratic error, her new house was head and shoulders above what she "deserved." It was nothing compared to what she'd left in either Shanghai or Paris, but lovely in a different way. Stucco, narrow, overflowing with the furniture of her previous homes. The deep red of the *paduak* shading into black. Awnings on the windows and green bamboo screens on the verandah. There was a small patch of grass with a border of portulaca. Tired and worn, but an oasis in the midst of Communist ugliness, and the source of a great deal of envy on her neighbors' parts.

Her bedroom had a big window and a small recessed balcony overlooking the center courtyard and a pot of bamboo, a small pine and a prunus—known as the three friends for the way they kept green in cold weather.

Her things were stored the Chinese way: folded up in boxes, the boxes under beds or used as chairs in the housekeeper's room.

Something jumped loudly into the pond. The ripples lasted for minutes. While I watched for it to reappear, the image of another girl at school in Paris. "Watch me," she said, pulling me into the school kitchen. She lowered her lips to the tub holding the dirty dishes and drank. She wanted to be a saint.

By my visit in 1966, my mother's street had been renamed to commemorate a soldier who'd given his life trying to save a mule from an oncoming train.

We laughed about it together.

That visit we ate sugared ginger in the front yard and chose to avoid her excessive gratitude at my visit and my guilt in the face of that excess. I showed her a photo of Cam with her palm-tree pigtail. She touched the spray of hair with a finger. "I will die without seeing her," she said, and then looked towards the front gate, and told me that pigtails were holdovers from feudalism.

She took the political situation seriously. I reminded her that bound feet were symbols of feudalism, and suggested hers be cut off. This returned us to laughter.

Years later Chou Yuan wrote me a letter with the details: Which old friend had made Mother wear a necklace of Ping-Pong balls as punishment for the jewelry discovered in her dresser. Which search the peach tree did not survive. How every Thursday she'd

173

been invited to unclog sewer pipes with her hands.

They'd spat at her on the street. Thrown rocks. Took over her house. Glass and ceramic covered the floors. The garden became a wrestling pit.

They cut her hair.

She disappeared in February, Chou Yuan watching from behind the house. They found her body in September.

And the worst of my shame, then and later, was that at moments I'd found myself seduced by this Cultural Revolution. I still turned it over and over. Had the tenets of this movement been a transformation? Or the release of something pent-up and hidden all along? During an early visit to my mother I'd commented that we really weren't in a position to judge what the Communists were doing; could we really say that what they were doing wasn't best for their country?

My mother had reached across the table to hold my wrist. Yes, she had answered. She could say just that.

Now, I opened my fists in my lap. The child. The drama of her situation was like that seduction: competing with Cam, the formidable force of my own creation. What that prospect set loose in my body.

I felt hands on mine. I opened my eyes. Cameron was leaning over me. "Are you alright?" she said.

My hands had found their way to my hair. She tried to gentle them loose, talking quietly. Her sounds were soothing, and I relaxed my hands into hers. When she coaxed them down to my lap, grey hairs feathered between my fingers.

***

UNTITLED

A WOMAN KNEELING in the dirt, her head bowed to the ground. Half of her head shaved.

In the background, out of focus, a naked girl squats with her back to the camera playing with the scraps of hair.

***

After Grady left, Sumin went upstairs to get the stolen pages. Alice followed, and Sumin let her. Celine's door was closed. Another late rising. One was strange enough, but two?

She laid her ear against the wood.

"She's not in there," Alice said.

Sumin still had her ear to the door.

Alice turned the knob. "You want to come in?" she said.

It's already become their room, Sumin thought.

The bed was made, Celine's slippers beside it. Sumin sat on the edge and slid her socked feet into them.

Alice watched. "I hate waking up without someone in the room," she said.

Sumin flexed her toes inside the slippers. "So do I," she said.

There were two books on the bedside table. St. Augustine's *Confessions* and underneath, a composition book. The cover was a dusty blue and the pages were green.

Alice said it was Celine's diary.

"Oh," Sumin said.

They both stared at it.

"Do you keep a diary?" Sumin asked. That's nice, she thought. What am I going to do? Spy on a six-year-old?

"No," Alice said, standing on one foot. "I keep an art journal." She hopped. "My mom and I used to do it together. She's an artist."

"I know," Sumin said. "Did you bring it with you?"

"Yup," Alice said, drifting across the room to Celine's jewelry on the dresser.

"Would you show it to me?" Sumin asked.

"No," she said.

Alice put on a jade pendant, then glanced over her shoulder. "You can read the diary if you want," she said. "I won't tell."

Sumin said she didn't want to, but she listened for sounds downstairs. She put St. Augustine back on the table. Alice had taken the necklace off and was clipping two earrings to one ear.

The other book was almost full. Celine had marked her place with a paper clip.

They seemed to be random notes; pronouncements of the sort that Sumin was more than familiar with.

Paper with uniformity. Without it, one's work looks like the imperfect work of man.

Blah, blah, blah, Sumin thought. One summer she'd walked into the kitchen to find her mother reading her diary. Sumin had asked her what she thought she was doing, and her mother had tossed the book onto the table.

She'd remarked that only those suffering from some unfulfillment kept diaries.

Sumin flipped around some more.

Do what you do properly. Never torment oneself. Grow older and older, quieter and quieter, and finally, create something. Combine things that haven't been together before. Look at something until you see what else it is.

Out the window the horse in the side meadow was flicking his tail, his head bent to the grass.

Alice was wearing all of Celine's jewelry and was leaning against the dresser as if from the weight. The sun caught the gold and silver, and whole parts of her were obscured by sharp light.

"Horse," Sumin said, pointing.

Alice jingled over.

I worry too much.

Along the Seine, an acrobat in yellow.

Everywhere I see what I can use. It's not only that Sumin doesn't; it's that when she does, she can't determine what use to make of it. She's like the boy who says, "If I only had a leash, I'd attach my squirrel to it. If I only had a squirrel."

Her misery shines around her like a halo.

I am planning an exquisite life with that child.

The last two entries were this morning at four. She closed the book. She heard footsteps and the refrigerator opening. Glass jars clinked.

Alice was still at the window.

"Alice," Sumin said. "Has Celine talked to you about who she thinks you should live with?"

Alice shook her head.

It was impossible to tell whether she was telling the truth. Downstairs, something fell.

"Come on," Sumin said, standing up. "Let's go. Take that stuff off."

Alice headed to the dresser, took everything off and left it in a pile.

Sumin stacked the books the way she'd found them, and restored the bedspread under the pillows with little karate chops. She told Alice to put the jewelry back the way she had found it.

Alice stirred the pile around. "I want to call my mother," she said.

"Fix the jewelry, and then we'll call," Sumin said.

Alice went to work and Sumin waited, turning things over in her head. She'd been preparing to come up against her daughter, which seemed daunting enough. But her mother. Her whole life she'd been coming up against the both of them with the same results: a humiliation or something close to it.

Cam walked me back to the house. Once satisfied that I wasn't going to die, she talked mostly about herself. Art school, her teachers, her fellow students. It didn't matter. I was glad to be excused from speaking. My heart was still racing and I was thankful for an arm to lean on.

The haze had never burned off. The trees lining the path maintained some grey.

Cam went on. She'd felt at home for the first time in art class.

I registered the insult.

People had liked her. They'd been interested in her opinions, in the way she saw the world.

She looked at me. I nodded. We walked in silence for a while. My breathing seemed noticeable. I wheezed at the end of exhales.

Talking about herself made her accelerate. I kept having to tug her gently back to my seventy-five-year-old pace. I said, "A noise woke me this morning and I thought I was back in the Shanghai house, in the bedroom with the celadon vase. There were other memory shards I couldn't place: two high heels in an empty hallway, the smell of baked pears, a staircase overgrown with wild grapevines."

Cam took her arm away to rub the shaved hair at the nape of her neck. "Mmm," she said. "I never sleep well when Alice is in the bed."

I tried to focus on walking in a straight line. "I sleep like never before," I said.

She didn't respond, and she didn't reoffer her arm.

Other memories I *had* placed: a midnight-blue jacket embroidered in gold thread, butterfly buttons up the left side, the envy of my Parisian schoolmates.

Sleeping with a clothespin on my nose, wishing to wake up looking less like my mother.

Cam was now on about what she really needed. More people to see her work; more sales.

"Especially now," she said, glancing sideways at me. "You know, with finances being such an issue."

"What?" I said.

"Because of Alice," she said, trying to contain her usual impatience.

"Therefore," I said, "if you didn't have Alice, you could stop worrying about finances."

We continued our walk. I added financial security to my mental list of reasons Alice would be better off with me. A benefit of my age. There were so many drawbacks.

Cam at twelve: just like the revolution. A transformation, or the release of something pent-up and hidden all along?

"Have you been listening to anything I've been saying?" I asked.

Cam nodded, her impatience palpable. "Pears. Grapes. I heard."

I looked at the path ahead of us.

"Celine," Cam said. "You're seventy-five." She paused. "You're getting old," she added.

"I understood what you meant," I said.

We were nearing the rock where I'd left

the camera and tripod. I began to plan my explanation. I intensely disliked the obligation I felt to offer one. Especially to her. "Pointing out my age is not the best strategy for getting favors from me," I said.

She slowed. "What is?" she asked. Her voice was soft, genuinely anxious. She really wanted this. But for herself, not for the child.

Gnats swarmed us. I waved them away from her head. "You're not suited for this role," I said. "You know this."

She was quiet, pulling in the corner of her lower lip the way she did before crying.

"You are not a mother," I said. "I did not raise you to be a mother. You're a model; the vessel of viewers' feelings, not the caretaker of those feelings."

Now, there were tears, slow and quiet. "You seem to be feeling better," she said. Her voice was strong. "Did it ever occur to you that what you raised me to be was not what I've become?"

"Of course your classmates, your teachers liked you," I said. "The exotic object is easy. The discipline of a mother is difficult."

Twigs broke under our feet.

"You should revel in what you are," I said.

I put a hand to her chin to make her look at me. Her face was her old face from our shoots. I was flushed with the recapturing.

"And why are you exotic?" I asked. She was staring at me, her black eyes trying to do damage. The look thrilled me. "Because of me." Adrenaline traveled to my extremities. The attribute she loved most about herself was the reason she would lose this battle.

She pulled loose and took a few steps backwards. Her hands were palm-up by her sides. Her face was nothing I knew. "What *am* I? What have I *got*?" she said.

She tried to go on. "I *know* I don't deserve this."

She broke off and I stood there, dumb, trying to refigure this person into the Cam I thought I knew. She walked off down the path.

I was still there when she returned, the camera in one hand, the tripod in the other. Her face was settled.

She held them out. "Drop these?" she asked.

She put them on the ground by my feet. "I'm gonna do this," she said. "Whether you help or not." She came closer and took both my hands in hers. "I may *not* deserve this, but neither do you," she said. She brought our hands to her cheek. "And another thing—everything you are is because of me."

❧

When they got downstairs, Cam was sitting at the kitchen table. Across the room, the refrigerator door was open.

"You left the door open," Alice said.

Cam didn't respond, which was so unusual that at first her mother didn't get it.

Alice retreated to a chair, keeping an eye on her.

Sumin looked out the sliding doors. "What have you done with Grady?" she asked.

Cam seemed not to have heard. She picked at her eyebrows, pulling the hairs out one by one. It was an alarming childhood habit.

Alice watched her, her tongue worrying her upper lip. "What are you doing?" she finally asked.

Cam came to. She turned to Alice. "How are you?" she asked.

"Good," Alice said, curling the place mat into a tube.

"What have you been up to?" Cam asked.

Sumin held still.

"Nothing," Alice said. She unrolled the place mat and asked Sumin whether she could call now.

Sumin nodded and on her way to the phone palmed the back of her daughter's head. "Are you having a bad day?" Sumin asked.

Alice asked where the phone was.

"It's coming," Sumin said. "Do you know the number?" she asked.

Cam ducked away from Sumin's touch. "I'll get it," she said.

Alice dug around in her pocket and came up with a carefully folded piece of yellow paper. "I have the number," she said.

Sumin shrugged at both of them and went to sit by the window.

Alice dialed. Cam stood next to her. They waited. Sumin could hear the ringing from across the room. Someone answered.

"Um, yes," Alice said. "Mommy?"

Sumin turned to Cam. "She talks to her mother in English?"

Cam didn't answer. "Ask for Shen Pei Rung," she said to Alice.

Alice did—in Chinese—and they all waited some more.

Sumin imagined a shared phone in the courtyard of some compound, a neighbor shuffling his way to the right door, the black receiver lying off the hook on a rickety wooden telephone table.

Alice came to attention. "Mommy?" she said. "Mommy," she said again, the one word filled with relief and nervousness and something close to happiness.

Cam stood still, listening. Sometimes she played with Alice's hair.

Alice spoke a mix of Chinese and English. Yes, Alice said. No. Yes. She looked around. *San*, she said, counting to three on her fingers. No, she said.

"Mommy," she said again. She seemed to be interrupting another question. "I'm a little worried," she said. She listened for a moment, then said something in Chinese. Then, "Well, I miss you." She listened again, nodding, but not saying anything. "But when?" she asked. Another pause. "But how long is that?"

Sumin felt suddenly awkward. She got Cam's attention and gestured her over. "Listen," she said quietly. "I have to tell you about something."

Cam was still focused on Alice's conversation.

Sumin touched her daughter's hand. "Give her some privacy," she said.

Cam didn't answer, but she did sit down in the chair next to her mother's.

Sumin tried again. "So," she said. "What's your sense of how Celine is feeling about this?" She nodded towards Alice.

Cam shrugged.

Sumin went on. "It might be that she's going to be more resistant than you thought."

Cam crossed her legs and looked at her mother. "Since when have you become an expert on Celine?" she said, and resumed her watch over Alice.

Alice was telling her mother again that she didn't like it here. She asked again why they couldn't go back to their old apartment in New York together.

If this conversation is hard for me, Sumin thought, what must it be like for Cam? She was moved by her own generosity until she realized she hadn't thought at all about how hard the phone call must've been for Alice's mother. She tried to recall the woman's image from the photo on Cam's dresser. All she could see was her own image staring back at her, and in a sudden rush she felt an overwhelming need to protect Alice's mother from the kind of heartache Cam could cause.

She reached over and rubbed one of her daughter's earlobes gently. "It's just that you might need to be better prepared than you thought you would." She was caught between sympathy and competitiveness.

Cam shook her head away from her mother's hand. "And what do you know about being prepared?" she asked. "I'm going to take lessons from you on how to deal with Celine, on how to be a mother?"

Alice was crying. Cam went over to her and rubbed circles across her back.

Sumin stood up. "At least I am a mother," she said quietly.

And on her way out of the room, that's what she was thinking. Celine may have made the photographs, but she'd made Cameron.

⌐☙

I was very ill the year we moved to Paris. Perhaps the first signs of the tuberculosis. In the meantime, I was given baths in a red copper tub lined with several cotton sheets. My mother's hands, winding my braid atop my head. Four arms lifted me up. The soap was English, black, smelling of tar and sheep.

I continued to shiver long after I'd been dried and put to bed. From the bed I could watch the servants empty the water from the tub, first by the bucketful, then finally with small silver ladles.

⌐☙

*S*umin watched them head towards the pond from her bedroom window. Alice kept lifting a hand to wipe her face. Cam put an arm around her, and they walked like that until Sumin couldn't see them anymore.

A few minutes later, Sumin was still at the window to see Celine heading towards the house. She walked out to meet her, wondering along the way where in God's name Grady was. Celine dropped the camera and the tripod at her feet and kept walking.

Sumin took a few steps to follow, and asked, "Hey, don't you want these?"

"Why don't you mind your own business?" Celine said, without turning around.

In her best moments, she told herself her mother was just trying to get by, like the rest of the world. In bad ones, she thought: Go ahead, create your own life, and leave me out of it. In her worst, she remembered that she had.

"I can create my own life," Sumin said loudly, trying to forget that she had gone from receiving money from her mother to receiving money from Grady.

Celine took an exaggerated step over the doorsill and disappeared. Sparrows bathed and chattered in the rainwater caught in the gutters. Sumin in the grass touched her forehead, then her eyes, then her lips, as if searching for the place where courage might be found.

———

A NAKED ONE-YEAR-OLD sitting on a stone wall. One hand rests on the stone. The other touches the woman's hands that frame her face.

The girl is crying. Her eyes shine and her mouth is open. Only the woman's hands and forearms are visible. Her tendons and ligaments are in sharpest focus.

Five minutes I was in my bedroom, on my bed, before Sumin came creeping around.

She, too, wanted something. She wanted to talk about how she might go about doing something she wanted to do.

I said, "How well put," and told her there would always be those who asked, "How?" while others acted.

She persisted. As if my response had been something she was resigned to in advance. I watched. She'd never been friendly with life. Probably her impotence had turned her against it.

She took half a step towards the chair, another step back.

I said, "Sit down, Sumin."

She sat. She moved to stand up.

"Stay," I said.

She sat.

"Do you ever try," she said, "even absent-mindedly, to put yourself in my place?"

I sighed. "I remember in Paris, having always to pass a broad and unremarkable street, as long as its name: Ver-cin-gé-to-rix." I looked at her until she looked at me. "This is what conversation with you is like." Clarifying her place made me begin to feel better.

She just smiled. It was not the response I was after.

"Am I meant to be moved by the sight of you?" I asked. I sat up and placed a pillow behind me. "Some people give their lives to others, and some to art. One is as unselfish as the other."

"*I* have an idea," Sumin said.

I closed my eyes. "Oh, for God's sake. How old are you? Should I congratulate you?"

She was quiet.

"If you have an idea—fine. You feel. You do. That's it. No explication."

"I need help," she said. "Or permission...," she faltered. "Or both."

I leaned back into the pillows. It felt good; relief without knowing my body needed it. "But of course you do."

She leaned forward in her chair, one hand on each knee. She began. "We both know Cam can't take care of Alice," she said.

"Of course," I said. I was pleased she'd inadvertantly brought an image of the child to my eye.

She wanted to raise Alice, and wanted my help to do it.

"How is it," I finally said, "that I spawned all these women who think they have what it requires to be a mother?"

She was quiet.

"I'll decide what's best for that child," I said. "And the rest of you will live with that decision."

She stood up straight, though she was picking at her nails. "Like you decided what was best for me?" she asked. "Like you decided for Cameron?"

She amused me. I said, "Look, my dear. If this is what you want, you do what you have to."

She shook her hands is if releasing them from a cramp.

"Of course you've never known how to go about things," I said. "You've kept yourself under anesthetic."

She was nodding her quick little nods that indicated she just wanted to go.

"Look," I said. "If you want to capture the creature, understand it; fashion a method by which you finally come to trap it."

She moved for the door. Her hand was on the knob. "Forget it," she said. "Forget I asked."

I waited.

"Do you want anything from downstairs?" she asked.

"There," I said. "There's the Sumin I know."

She took her hand from the doorknob and wiped her cheek. "Celine," she said. "How did your mother die?"

It was as if she'd thrown a sandbag onto my chest.

She was standing there, but when I tried to think of what to say, there was nothing.

Finally, she said, *"Wu ji bi fan,"* and left, closing the door behind her.

An old phrase, resurrected during the Cultural Revolution. I'd heard my mother use it: *When things can get no worse, they must get better.*

❧

*S*umin was back in her room before she let her breath out. She hadn't realized she was holding it. She closed her door, and leaned against it.

For the first time, she felt herself to be like her mother, and the shock unmoored her; she was a piece of cloth dipped in water.

If she wanted to capture the creature, she had to understand it; find out something about it, and fashion a method by which she could finally come to trap it.

Thursday

$\mathcal{A}$lice was gone when I woke, her place in the bed already cool. It had been her worst night yet. While we'd still been downstairs, she'd been out of bed five or six times looking for us. The Cookie Monster cup had not helped. Finally, Grady had gone upstairs and sat with her until she fell asleep. Later, she'd whimpered her way through the night; her arms and legs moved in long, graceful motions. Nothing about it had been restorative.

I kept this to myself at breakfast and no one asked about her. Where had she gone? Breakfast had involved Cam pretending to read the newspaper with Grady looking from her to me to her—the oaf detective sure that *some*thing was going on right under his nose. Sumin was missing as well. Were they together? Where?

I escaped to my studio, distracting myself with old prints. Rejects. There were plenty. I'd always followed Watts' advice: "What is, is, and one should not desire to make it seem to be other."

Still, I took some pleasure in them.

A shadow outside disappeared as I focused on it. Where could they be?

"Talking to yourself again?" Cam asked from the doorway. Grady was lurking behind her.

It was clear that whatever information Sumin thought she had, she'd gotten from him. To me fell the task of having to ferret out what he knew. I let them in.

They sniffed around the studio. I resisted asking about Sumin and Alice.

They concluded their tour at a warped and interesting print of twelve-year-old Cam in profile. Her head against the top rung of a ladderback chair, her face greased with shaving cream. Hands held a straight edge to her jawline.

The size of the Big Character Posters of the Cultural Revolution had always made sense to me. My own prints had always been eight-by-ten or larger. Usually sixteen-by-twenty. A power came from magnifying.

Grady broke the silence. "Whose hands?" he asked.

"Sumin's," Cam said. "Remember how pissed she was?" she said more to herself than to either of us. She sat in the armchair.

We'd always been able to reach some degree of reconciliation by way of Sumin.

"They look like the hands you've been sketching," Grady murmured.

"Yeah, right," Cam said.

I almost smiled.

Grady put the print aside and looked at

the next one. Cam stared out the window. Her lack of interest was unusual.

Manchu Princess: Her face made up with pink and white Manchu powder to appear as oval as possible, like a melon seed. The headdress of pearl strands and kingfisher and peacock feathers had never quite worked out. Her artificial long red nails were curved around the grappling hook I'd suspended from the center beam. She was naked.

"The naked body contains the flaws of the person," I mused to myself.

"Stop speaking in edicts," Cam said.

"It's how I speak," I said.

She'd shown friends the advance copies of *Twelve.* The girls had bent over the book, their arms crossed low over their stomachs. Cam *had* enjoyed being envied.

"Does Sumin look anything like your mother?" Grady asked.

"No," I said.

"That's not true," Cam said. "She does a little—especially now that she's getting older."

"You never met my mother," I told her.

"But she's seen pictures, surely," Grady said.

Cam was restless. She stood and tapped out a syncopation on the developer trays. She hiked herself onto the table.

A sound outside. Cam and I both turned to the window. Nothing. We caught, then dropped, each other's eyes.

I needed to sit. I left Grady to the prints and took Cam's place in my armchair.

She was swinging her legs back and forth. Her leg muscles contracted, relaxed. The developing trays shivered with each swing. She studied me. "Grady," she said. "Tell Celine what a fabulous mother you think I am."

Grady looked up, the baffled sloth. Any European elegance I may have seen in him before was gone. "Well," he stuttered, "she is...I mean, she will be." He glanced at Cam, who was still looking at me. "She is," he said again.

I held Cam's stare. "That little idea seems to have backfired," I said.

She wouldn't look at him.

"You are not a fabulous mother," I said. "And you're unlikely to become one."

Grady wondered whether I wasn't being harsh.

"First," I said. "A mother never worships beauty. It's particularly narrow. And second, a mother can't become infatuated with self-love at the expense of self-examination."

Cam stopped swinging her legs and pointed a finger at me. "Hey," she said. "You're not talking about *my* problem."

I had no idea what she was talking about, but even Grady was behaving as if I'd said something horribly ironic.

Where was Alice? I was hot and dizzy. I wanted to sit in a cool room and share a glass of tea.

Would-be artists, I began, not knowing how I would finish the sentence. They saw nothing, because they didn't know their traditions. They spent their time reading books about art rather than looking at the world.

I said to Cam, "Do you know Carroll? Do you know Weston?"

She stood up. "What are you talking about?" she said.

This was embarrassing. "You don't even know your namesake."

She took a step towards me. She was furious. Would she hit me? I wondered, almost thrilled. "I am not *talking* about photographers," she said.

Grady got between us.

Cam ran her hands through her hair and held them there. "Are you going to help me or not?" she asked.

"You and your mother want the same things," I said, standing. "She has her ways of trying to get what she wants, and you have yours. You both think these are things you're entitled to. Nobody helped me."

She seemed to have stopped listening. "What do you mean we both want the same things?" she said.

I pushed past Grady and began putting away the prints. "She hasn't told you," I said. "How characteristic."

"Told her what?" Grady asked.

"She wants Alice," I said.

There was a large silence. I turned around. The light coming through the front windows banded her legs.

She must have seen how I was looking at her.

She was calm. "I'm sorry," she said inexplicably, and went to the door.

"I won't help you with Alice," I said. Something seemed suddenly lost.

"I will tell you this," I said, but she was outside and closed the door behind her. Instead, I gave myself the advice I would've given her: Only try to describe the things you've seen. Look harder at the things that cause you pain.

❧

$\mathcal{S}$umin sat balanced on the fence of the riding ring watching Alice go around in circles on a good-natured pony. Sumin could hear the music from the Central Park carousel as if it were playing right now, and she remembered a detail Celine had shared from her adolescence in Paris: a steam merry-go-round in almost every quarter. The one nearest her house had no horses. Instead, fire engines, boats, cars and a white rabbit in full gallop.

The trainer held the lunge line, calling out instructions in a calm voice. Alice was good at following them. She sat up straight, she pushed her heels down, turned in her toes, closed her hands gently over the reins and followed the movements of the pony's head. She couldn't stop smiling, and Sumin thought if she did nothing else right this whole trip, it would still be a good week.

❧

They were in the kitchen when I returned to the house. Alice was dirty and sweaty. Sumin was pleased with herself.

"I rode a horse," Alice announced. "Well, a pony, but a pretty tall pony." She gestured above her head.

I wiped grit from her cheek. "I'm so glad for you," I said. "It must've been exciting."

"I'm very good at it," she said. She asked for iced tea. The pitcher was on the counter, next to Sumin, who was washing dishes.

Sumin said, "She really is. You should've seen her."

I moved around her and dumped the tea down the drain.

"Celine, those were clean," Sumin said.

You do not know how to make tea, I told her.

I filled the kettle and put it on to boil. I got a new pitcher from the cupboard. I got more tea bags, lemons. She was underfoot every step of the way. Alice sat at the table, drifting, smiling to herself.

I dropped four tea bags into the pitcher with lemon slices as thin as tissue paper. I lifted them with my nails so as not to ruin their perfect shape. The curve of the pitcher, the form and the eye of the antelope.

"Water's boiling," Sumin said.

I poured.

"She really loved it," Sumin said.

"Where's my tea?" Alice asked, coming to.

Sumin said she would have to wait a minute. I carried the pitcher out onto the porch. I found a sunny corner for it. Yesterday's haze was gone. The afternoon light was raw silk. I looked forward to the sunset.

Sumin came out and sat facing the sun, squinting at me. "She was happier than she's been all week," she said.

Two thumps inside.

"Alice?" I called. "What are you doing?"

"Taking off my shoes," she said.

We listened for more noises.

"I can do this," Sumin said.

Our friend the cat emerged from under the house and peered up at me. "No," I said. "You can't." This caused a short silence.

"Should I ask Grady about your mother?" she said.

"How is that supposed to affect me?" I said.

She said nothing, as if she had nothing to do but wait for my response.

"What is it you think you know?" I said.

"Here it is," she said. "I can ask you questions, or I can talk to Grady."

We both turned. Grady and Cam were on the path making their way towards us. Neither waved. It looked like they were deep in conversation without any words.

They were halfway to the house. Before they arrived, I said to her, "Don't pursue this. It's ugly. It's pointless. And it's beneath even you."

$\mathcal{S}$umin surprised Grady by meeting him at the top of the stairs with a kiss. "I missed you," she said.

Cam peered around him from the step below. Her eyelashes were wet. "Where's Alice?" she said. "Forget it," she said before Sumin could answer.

Sumin shrugged, and Cam pushed past both of them and went into the house. As she passed him, Grady squeezed her shoulder.

Whatever *that's* about, Sumin thought and moved to kiss him again, but he was already on the move, and she went left when she should've gone right, and ended up kissing ear.

Grady said, "What do you want?" He glanced at Celine, who was gazing off the porch as if alone.

Sumin fixed the collar of his shirt and left her hand on his chest. "I don't *want* anything. Can't I just kiss you and tell you I missed you?"

He didn't take her hand away. "It's not that you can't," he said. "It's that you don't."

She took her hand away, and he went inside. She followed him into his room.

She hadn't been in it since Tuesday. It looked the same. Some of the accordian folders had been rearranged. She wondered if he'd identified all of the missing pages.

She sat on the couch. He fiddled with his computer. She watched.

"What are you doing?" he asked.

"Nothing. Are you going to work?" she said.

He turned off his computer. "No, actually."

"Oh," she said.

They looked at each other. He got up and went to the door.

"Where are you going?" she asked. "Maybe we could go for a swim."

He held it open. "I'm going to do more modeling for Cam," he said. "She didn't get everything she needed yesterday."

They could hear her moving around upstairs, singing a children's song.

"What have you guys been talking about anyway?" Sumin asked.

"A lot of things," he said. He glanced towards the stairs. "You should ask her to tell you about it."

Ha! Sumin thought, but she knew he was trying to help.

She joined him by the door. "Where are you going to do the modeling?" she asked.

He put his hands in his pockets. "I don't know. Down by the pond."

They stood there for a second. He said, "I don't think Cam wants you to see the portrait before Saturday."

"Have you?"

He shook his head. Cam appeared, singing, but not enjoying herself. She slung her big bag over her shoulder. "Ready?" She didn't look at her mother.

"Sumin was thinking of coming," Grady said.

"I don't think so," Cam said.

Grady looked pained.

"What is going on with you two?" Sumin asked, exasperated.

Grady looked at Cam, waiting for her cue.

She didn't give him one, except to leave the room.

Sumin appealed to him. He told her they should probably talk later, and then he left, too.

Perfect, Sumin thought. "You should be embarrassed," she called after him.

Sumin went into the kitchen. Her mother was getting a glass of water. Alice was drawing more horses.

"You're talking to yourself?" Celine asked. She took two containers of pills from her pocket and tapped out a capsule from each.

"Are you alright?" Sumin asked.

Celine swallowed both pills at once and made a face. "I'm old. I take pills."

"Does Cam seem okay to you?" Sumin asked.

"Why?" Celine said, holding the glass of water out in front of her.

The seriousness with which her mother had greeted her question took her by surprise. "No reason," she said.

They held each other's stares for a minute, then let them drop.

"We're going swimming," Sumin said.

"We are?" Celine said.

"No. We—Alice and I," she said.

Alice looked up. "We are?" she said.

Celine walked to the stairs. She held the bannister and climbed slowly back to her room. "Have a good time," she said. It sounded like she meant it.

~

There was no use telling anyone about the fainting. In a few days I would be seventy-five. Born in the Year of the Hare. Believed to inhabit the moon, pounding the elixir of life at the base of a cassia tree. Known for our large, lustrous eyes and an uncanny clear-sightedness. More easily moved by personal problems than global ones. More than anything else, we prize our comfort and security, and we'll have it on one condition: that we keep away from the dramatic situation, the insurmountable obstacle. The female Hare is said to become with young by licking the fur of the male. She is said to produce her young from the mouth. Before I left Paris, I looked up what kind of relationship the Hare-mother was meant to have with the Rat-child. Alice's sign. "To be avoided like the plague," the chatty American book read.

I sat up for another sip of water. The room tipped.

The pencil case for school, wooden with a landscape on its front, a scene of snow and sleighs. I'd scraped the scene off with my letter opener, wanting to see how the paint got onto the wood.

I was sweating and nauseous. I knocked

over my glass. Water splashed the bedside table. The glass rolled to the edge of the wall and stopped with a thud.

Where was everyone?

My mother's words about anything that went wrong: *meiyoubanfa*. Nothing could be done. It was hopeless.

❧

UNTITLED

A YOUNG WOMAN in traditional Japanese wedding dress. A bright embroidered kimono. Fabric-covered wire flowers angle out from her hair. There are grooves in the hair, as if it's been sculpted with a wide-toothed comb.

In front of the woman, a pedestal table. On it, a porcelain sake pitcher the shape of an hourglass. Light spots reflect off its curves. Next to the jar, three shallow drinking saucers. The fourth is raised to the woman's lips. Her hands cradle it, index fingers and thumbs on the rim. Her eyes on the liquid she sips.

To her left, barely discernible, a man from neck to mid-thigh. Bigger than she is, even from that perspective. He is the groom, out of focus, in Western dress.

❧

Cam and Grady were set up under the willow. Grady was on the bench with Cam on the grass in front of him, her back to the pond.

They were delighted to see Alice. But they looked at Sumin as if embarrassed for her. It was exactly the look Cam's father had given Sumin when she told him she was pregnant. Now that she was there, she knew she wouldn't try to make them tell her what was going on.

Alice chattered about her riding lesson while Sumin worked around her, undressing her, coating her with lotion, holding her suit for her to step into.

Cam took the suit from Sumin's hands. "I'd really prefer you weren't here," she said.

"How nice," Sumin said.

"I don't want you to see the portrait," Cam said. The portrait was nowhere to be seen.

Sumin rubbed the excess lotion onto the back of Alice's neck. "Alice wanted to go swimming," she said. "You weren't around." She told Alice she'd show her how to do an underwater handstand. Alice said that she might try that later and settled herself at the edge of the pond, squatting to draw in the wet sand.

Sumin floated around near shore, splashing around whenever she went by the happy little group. She treaded water for a while, listening in.

"Are you okay?" Grady asked, and Sumin thought he was talking to her, but Cam answered.

"I don't know," she said.

The water lapped at Sumin's chin. A swarm of tiny somethings materialized. She flailed her arms quietly.

Alice looked up, then resumed drawing.

Sumin breaststroked in a little circle. She got closer to them and floated on her back, her eyes closed. Her hands did small figure eights just under the surface.

"Well, that's one thing Celine *has* given me," Cam said. "Built-in defenses. When you live your life like she has, I guess you need them."

"What do you mean?" Grady asked. Both women looked up at the change in his tone.

Cam shrugged. "She's an *artiste*," she said.

Then it was quiet.

Sumin righted herself, and moved towards shore until her feet touched the soft bottom. She sat next to Alice and studied the drawing. She reached over and added a swirl.

"Let her do her own drawings," Cam said.

Alice said it was okay. Cam repeated herself.

Sumin coughed and walked over to her towels. She wrapped one around her hair, turban-like, and the other around her waist. She sat, her knees pulled up. "She was always allowed to nix the ones she didn't like," she said, apropos of nothing.

The two of them looked at her.

She leaned back on her hands. The grass tickled her palms. "The photos. She always had veto power," she said.

She lay down on her back, her sneakers under her head as a pillow.

I should just leave, she thought. I should just go back to the house.

"What I said about envy?" Cam said to Grady. "It doesn't apply to my mother."

"Why do you two do this?" Grady said. "Can't you try to make things easier for each other?"

Cam flipped her sketchpad closed, got up and leaned over her bag, stuffing things in it. "Come on, Alice. We're going."

Alice stood up, her sandy fingers spread wide by her sides. She rinsed her hands off and gathered her things.

Cam helped her. "In the past two years, my mother has tried sales, movie producing, romance novels, bartending and freedom marches." She slung her bag over her shoulder and reached for her sandals with her foot. "She'd call to tell me the latest, and I'd say: 'That sounds good,' or, 'Why not?' " She got both her sandals on and stood in front of Grady. "And she'd go on and I'd zone out, trying to imagine a life without 'my latest identity' phone calls from Sumin."

Sumin wanted her to stay, the way an alcoholic's wife wants him to stay an alcoholic.

Cam started walking towards the path. "And now she wants to try 'mother,' get it right this time." She took Alice's hand. "Well, I'm not going to help again with that little experiment," she said. "I think I've given enough to that cause."

Sumin watched them disappear. She heard Alice ask what they were talking about. It sounded as if Cam answered, "Nothing. Just me and my screwed-up life."

Grady came down to sit next to her. He was sixty-five, but nothing about him seemed frail.

208

For a second it seemed like he was going to pick her up. "She's not what you think she is."

Sumin didn't answer.

"You guys should talk to each other," he said.

Sumin didn't want to think about this. "Do you remember," she said, "how when you were first in love with me, you were aggressively uninterested in getting to know my family?"

She looked at him. "You drew a circle in the air with your hand. You said, 'This is not about all of us; this is about us.' "

He nodded.

"I guess you talked to Celine," she said.

He said, "Why didn't you tell me about wanting Alice?"

She shrugged. "I wasn't really sure."

"Are you now?" he asked.

She nodded. "As sure as you were when you wanted to adopt," she said.

He took her hand from her lap and laced their fingers. He used their two hands to turn her face to his and then he drew a line in the air from her mouth to his and back again.

The tenderness of the gesture made her collapse from the inside. She started crying. What he would be most concerned with hadn't even crossed her mind.

"I'm sorry," he said. "I always wanted to pay you the kind of attention I thought you deserved. I'm sorry," he said again.

She kissed him.

"Is it just Alice that you want?" he asked. "Or Alice and me?"

She leaned into him. She had another thought that made her shiver.

He hugged her tighter. He rubbed her shoulders and she kept coming back to how to make getting information from him easier.

The notion of irrevocably altering Celine and Cam's positions in the family floated around her. Here was her leash and squirrel.

And what about Alice, she thought. Wasn't she supposed to be thinking about Alice?

You're sick, she thought, shivering again. You get exactly what you deserve.

Friday

So she slept with him. On the sofa in his room, flanked by his laptop and his fax, with the accordian folders filled with his notes spilling over onto the floor from their passion. During the lovemaking, her fingers found the folders.

By mid-morning, she'd sent him on errands in town, shopping for the next day's birthday dinner and checking on the VW. Celine and Alice were still in bed. Before Cam had disappeared with her sketchbook, Sumin had asked if they were ever going to talk about this; Cam hadn't answered in a way that made Sumin more worried than insulted. So, she was now cross-legged on Grady's couch, a new folder spread across her lap.

End of August 1967—end of September/The Red Terror. Home raids, beatings—suicides. Estimates: 1,700 in Beijing. 33,600 homes raided/84,000 guilty of the Four Olds and driven out of town.

Biantian zhang—documents the Guards accused people of keeping as secret reminders of their former glories.

The note had been boxed in by doodling.

Good Art served workers, peasants and soldiers. Bad Art created to celebrate intellectual activity.

She savored the understanding that under this definition, Celine's art was bad. "Bad, bad, bad," she said, flexing the cramp from her right foot.

She pulled free a bundle of papers fastened with a binder clip. A yellow Post-it stuck to the first page: *Mao.* She leafed through it.

Just his thoughts could perform miracles:

Surgery patients not anesthetized. Instead given Little Red Book and instructed to shout, "Long Live Chairman Mao." In revolutionary frenzy they would feel no pain.

Instead of morning breaks for workers, a "ballet of loyalty": improvisational dance in which they were to use their bodies to demonstrate loyalty to Mao.

For teeth: Chairman's Hardy Pine toothpaste.

If she hadn't known where it had led, she could've found it funny. She skimmed the rest of the bundle, growing more impatient. What did all this have to do with them?

Finding things like details from the Cultural Revolution funny was *why* she didn't have anyone to share her life with, she thought. Grady's clothes from last night were in a little heap at the end of the sofa. She pushed them with her toes. She put her fingers between her legs and then held them up to her nose. One of her favorite things about making love was that afterwards her own smell was so much stronger.

A hand still up to her nose, she went back to the bundle.

On May Day 68, fifty-one executed. Fifty-one because of 5/1. On National Day, October 1, 101.

Another Post-it: *Suicides.* Sumin sat up and peeled it off. She stuck it on her leg for the time being.

Slogans on the pavement where the body had landed: "Good riddance, traitor. Even death cannot pay for your sin," etc. See Spence.

She realized she didn't have any idea *how* Huying had killed herself. She reread Grady's note and tried to imagine the Huying she knew about jumping out a window or hanging herself or swallowing a handful of pills. All the options seemed equally feasible and equally ridiculous. All she'd ever heard was how strong she was. She read on. She only had to go a few pages before she hit an answer: *Death from beatings labeled suicides.*

She closed her eyes. You imbecile, she thought. "You know nothing," she said out loud.

There were sounds from the kitchen. The door was closed, but not locked. She sank lower on the couch and held still. Catch me, she thought. Right here, right now. It must've been Celine or Alice poking around in the cabinets. She had the urge to call out. The sounds stopped.

She looked back through the notes, turning pages quietly.

In Grady's handwriting next to the note: *See: Specifics/Family.*

She got up and went to the desk, scanning Grady's papers. Again, his system was a mystery. She found the folder, sat at the desk and made her way through it, piling the looked-through pages to her right.

On house fronts, posters written by children severing all relationships with their capitalist parents.

Parents turned in by children rode buses together to denunciation meetings.

Li? Check s's: Artist's daughter, after Guards' first search, gathered up father's art supplies and turned him in. When he killed himself, she spat on his coffin and said, "Suicide. Betrayer of the people, betrayer of the Party."

Why had Grady treated this information this way? So what if Huying had been beaten to death? Wasn't the result the same?

cf. Yellow Feet.

Those who tried to draw a clear line between themselves and their parents gained nothing from their betrayal. It was as if they had sold their souls and went unpaid.

The door opened. Cam.

Sumin stared at her, waiting.

"Have you seen Alice?" Cam asked.

Sumin shook her head.

Cam looked around as if checking her story.

"Isn't she in her room?" Sumin asked, turning the pages in her lap facedown.

"No," Cam said. "Celine hasn't seen her all morning. I thought you'd taken her somewhere again." She looked at the pages in her mother's lap.

"What's that supposed to mean?" Sumin asked.

"What are you doing in here?" Cam asked.

Sumin glanced around and stood up. The idea was to block her daughter's view. "Helping Grady out," she said.

"Mmm," Cam said. "Thought you weren't helping out on this one."

Sumin said, "Well, now I am."

Cam hiked her bag higher onto her shoulder. "Yeah, well, sex'll do that," she said.

Why do I ever worry about her? Sumin thought. "Do you want help looking?"

"No," Cam said. "I do not."

She walked to the desk and stared at the papers for a while. Sumin acted like she didn't care. "So," Cam said. "Find anything good?"

The second the question was out, Sumin knew that the best thing about the information she'd just discovered was that she didn't have to share it with Cam. She had something Cam didn't have, and though she didn't yet know how it would help, she knew it couldn't hurt her chances with Alice. She said, "Nothing much. Reviews. You know."

"Poor Sumin," Cam said. "Other people's accomplishments." She waited for a reaction, and then shrugged. "I hope the sex was good," she said, moving towards the door. "It's not going to help you get Alice."

"It was wonderful," Sumin said.

Cam left the door open behind her, and after she got all the way upstairs Sumin shut it and locked it. Then she unlocked it, realizing that its being locked would be impossible to explain.

Another hour of spying. The room was a mess. Grady would be back soon. She put on a shirt of his over her own. He liked it when she wore his clothes.

And then a small, crisp manila envelope. Inside, a single sheet of onion skin paper folded in half, single-spaced typing, at the head of the page: *Translated by Hsing Chiang, July 9, 1990.*

The ninth had been last Monday. It must've been the delivery Grady had stayed in the city for.

—*Sitting on an upturned bucket, the beaten earth as my desk, I write my confession.*

—*Hunger is our motif. My cellmate—a woman from Shanghai. Our fathers worked together.*

She thought she heard a car. She looked out at the driveway. She wondered if Cam had found Alice. How had Grady gotten a hold of whatever this was? He read Chinese pretty well. Why had he used someone else for the translation?

—*My body is nothing. Sex is nothing. A way to food. The guard's cheek against my breast for a sweet potato. His fingers between my legs for corn. He's oblivious to my age, my grotesque feet. My cellmate warned me to stop this trading. I ignored her. She died. I was on the detail to bury her.*

—*A butterfly today, circling my head. If two people cannot be together in this life, they will in the next. This is what this means. Li Na.*

Celine's Chinese name was so unfamiliar that

it took Sumin a second to remember it. How had Grady gotten this? Did Celine know about it? Did Cam?

—*The old myth that heaven cries for the unjustly taken lives of the young. But I am old. No home, no husband, no family. I chant to myself, while I work, while I am beaten, while the guard pushes his fingers around inside of me:* Si le hao, si le hao; si jiushi liao, liao jiushi hao.

The translator had put the Chinese in italics, the English following: Death is good, death is good; death is the end, the end is good.

Goose bumps rose on Sumin's arms and legs. She heard a crunching sound. Someone's dog was sniffing around on the driveway.

Couldn't Celine have done something? She was having trouble imagining her mother as powerless, even during the years of no work. Money had never been that tight.

—*I would change nothing. I would have Li Na change nothing. She would still give me her photographs—all of them. I would still receive them—all of them. I would still refuse to destroy them. And I would still—always and again—be here, in this place, because of them.*

At the bottom of the page, the notes were dated August 1967. Sumin had to stand up. She had to put things away. She did, paying no attention to precision. Papers went into the nearest folders. When she filled one, she started on another. She made no attempt to put the folders in their original places.

She spent the rest of the afternoon imagining the narrative that went with that thin white page.

She wondered again whether or not Celine knew all this already, and then, to keep herself from getting too excited, she reminded herself that she'd never in her whole life been better informed than her mother.

But mostly she went back to the earlier note about drawing a line between you and your family, selling your soul and not getting paid for it. She couldn't decide whom that note applied to best, Celine and her mother or herself and Cam. And with the attempt came the tiny and definite possibility of having discovered common ground with her mother. When she thought about whom she wanted to share that thrill with, if not now then later, she thought of Alice.

I was sharp with Alice this morning, and she held her hand to her mouth and left. So hours later, when Cam knocked and came in, I sat up, hoping not to look as poorly as I felt.

She was beautiful. With her came the smells of outdoors: honeysuckle and pond, moist heat.

"What are you doing?" she asked.

"Smelling you," I said.

She frowned.

She had hated compliments since she was a teenager. We wouldn't apologize. We never did.

"Have you seen Alice?" she said.

I didn't tell her about our morning exchange.

"Sumin is downstairs going through Grady's

218

stuff," she said. She went to the window and peered out. "Where is she?" she asked the window. "They had sex last night," she said.

The conversation was confusing me. I was trying to ascertain what she expected. The West believed the head controlled everything. Yet, you saw a lovely girl across a room and you walked towards her with hope in your mind. That was the way our pictures were made.

She seemed to be sliding away. "I suppose we have only the past in common now, and that can't last long," I thought. I realized I was speaking aloud.

"The first time I felt a man put his fingers inside of me it was like watching someone look through one of our books," she said.

She'd never talked with me like this. I tried to focus. What did this have to do with Alice?

"My insides were cold and smooth. He asked if I was alright, and I told him I was there, wasn't I? I was sixteen."

She was crying.

"You gave me away," she said. "You gave me to anyone who wanted to look." She wiped her face roughly with the back of her hand. She was instantly six.

"I used to think of you as an intruder," she said. "But then I knew intruders wanted something."

She came around to the side of the bed and stood over me. Her black hair picked up highlights from the white of the ceiling. She'd stopped crying.

"I used to think you had all the power. You

could pull me here, push me there, hand me out like a party favor. But there was an exact moment," she said, "during that last summer when I was twelve, when I realized the kind of power I held over you. When I knew I had what you needed."

Was this what had happened? I thought. Was this the moment that child's playfulness had given way to adult poise? What must I look like? I thought.

"If Sumin wants what you say she wants," she said, "then I need your help even more than before."

I listened for outside noises. Something to ground me. An unidentifiable buzzing.

Cam said, "Negotiating with Sumin is impossible for me; it always has been."

I was enveloped by the sensation of the past jostling the present. I anticipated one more chance to see Cam at her most intense. What would she do when she learned I too wanted the child?

"I admit I need your help," she said. "The least you can do is admit how much you once needed me. Admit you owe me this help now. At least this."

There was a line from Turgenev's *Virgin Soil*, a suicide note: "I could not simplify myself." Sumin thought there was nothing but difference between her and me; what she'd never understood was that without Cameron, that note could have been—would have been— my note. We all wanted Alice to offer us that help, that safety.

I could get nothing out. Inside, too much. A fragment from my mother's letter: *Today they asked me, "What can you be thinking about? What is it you pin your hope on?"*

Cam's hand was on my forehead. Her voice was swaddled. "I can't get myself back," she said. "I can't ever know what I would've been without you. I know that."

I closed my eyes.

"But Alice and I," she said, "we can help each other be better people. Be as much our own as the circumstances can allow."

My mother's funeral: I wailed like a professional mourner in the traditional fashion: "Ah, Mama, how could you so thoughtlessly leave us behind? Ah, Mama, do something good for us, take us with you." But no tears. Children's tears would bring suffering to the parent in the next world.

When I opened my eyes, Cam was gone. Her odor remained in the heavy air.

If my mother had denounced her family background, her husband, me, she would have had a chance. She refused. This was my comfort and my torture.

After she'd become a target of the Red Guards' interrogations, I'd written to her because I'd thought it would help her cause, once they read the letter: *It is very difficult to maintain our own lives. How can we relate when you still want to lead this kind of life? We've all drawn a clear line to separate ourselves from you. Learn from us.*

———

Untitled

A wide path cuts through rows of high corn. The plants stand straight, the tassels limp.

On the path, an adolescent girl. A wicker basket on her head. One arm holds the basket steady. She's wearing dark gym shorts with white piping. They're too big for her, and she's rolled the waistband. They're still low on her straight hips. She is naked from the waist up.

Behind her, to the right, an older man. He wears overalls and a long-sleeved shirt. His cap reads: Hook's Feed Store.

He has stopped the girl by placing a hand on her upper arm. She is partially turned to him. Her head and eyes tilt down at his dusty workboots. Her body leans away from him. She wears a small smile.

He is not smiling. His thumb and fingers press into her upper arm.

It is called The Pipa Lesson.

A stocky farmer sits in a metal folding chair on the grass. Behind him, the sun is setting. He is mostly silhouette.

On his knees, a small girl kneels, her back to him. She tilts her head back. Her hair falls across his face. His arm across her flat stomach like a bow.

When Grady got back, Celine summoned him from the top of the stairs.

He and Sumin were putting away groceries.

Sumin said, "I'll get this. You go on upstairs." She dropped a bag of rice. The plastic split down its seam. Rice skittered everywhere. He wiped his hands on his pants, shrugged and took the stairs two at a time.

"Perfect," she said, squatting to reach under the sink for dustpan and brush.

Cam came inside. She stepped over her mother, scattered rice on her way to the sink and got a glass of water.

Sumin reached over and held her ankle. "Be still," she said.

Cam pulled her ankle away roughly. She was wearing her painting clothes: red Converse high-tops, no socks, jean shorts, and a sleeveless denim shirt knotted at the waist. Her hair was kept out of her face with an elaborate system involving multiple bobby pins. Cam spent a lot of time looking like she had spent no time at all thinking about how she looked. She asked if Alice had come back.

Sumin looked up. "You still can't find her?" she said. "Have you looked?"

"Have you?" Cam asked.

"Hand me the garbage can," Sumin said.

Cam went to sit at the table. Rice now covered seven-eighths of the kitchen floor.

"Here," Sumin said. "You clean this up, and I'll go look."

Cam had her head in hands. "I don't think so," she said.

Upstairs, it sounded like they were arguing. "Is there a reason for this behavior?" Sumin asked.

Cam took a big swallow of water. "Don't be an idiot," she said.

Sumin put the dustpan down to study her. "Have you been looking for her or painting?"

"Both," Cam said.

Sumin snorted and resumed rice cleanup. "Whatever that means," she said. "Some mother," she said quietly.

"I must've missed your search parties," Cam said.

Sumin closed her eyes. Stop this, she thought. Just stop it.

Cam stood up. "I thought she might be down by the creek; she modeled for me there a couple of days ago."

Was everyone modeling for Cam? Sumin dumped the full dustpan into the garbage. Some of the rice missed the pail. "She wouldn't go there," Sumin said. "She didn't have a very good time. Did you check at the stables?"

Cam took her mother's head between her hands. They were cold, and Sumin recalled an early-morning shoot for *Six*: Celine breathing on Cam's hands to warm them.

"You need to back off on this one," Cam said.

She couldn't tell how much of Cam's tone was desperation. Their faces were very close. "Have you been crying?" Sumin asked.

Cam dropped her hands.

Sumin was blinking. Without realizing it, *she* had started to cry. She took a breath and a little sound came with it. She needed to make Cam understand how much she needed this child; Cam did not often lavish sympathy, least of all on her mother.

"Sumin," Cam said.

"I'm fine," Sumin said.

Alice arrived at the sliding door. She asked what was wrong with them.

Cam rushed over to her, patting her down as if frisking her. Alice ducked away. "What are you doing?" she said.

"Where have you been?" Cam demanded.

Sumin held out her hand. Alice came over and took it. "What did you do today?" Sumin asked.

"A lot," Alice said. She looked at the rice on the floor.

"Like what?" Sumin asked, picking leaves out of her hair.

Alice let go of Sumin's hand and opened the fridge. "Where's Celine?" she asked.

"Upstairs," Sumin said.

"Oh," Alice said. "I'm hungry."

"Get something to eat," Sumin said. She was still sad.

Alice hunted around in the fruit drawer. Cam said, "Listen, let's all go on a walk." She took her mother's arm. "Leave this for later." She gestured at the rice.

"Yes," Sumin said, wiping her face. "Let's do that."

Alice said she'd just been on a walk. She took a peach and followed them anyway.

They walked down the steps and onto the path. It was already late afternoon. The cicadas had started. Alice walked between them. Cam tried to get her to promise not to disappear again. She promised. Cam started a game that involved swinging Alice's arm in a circle.

While Sumin watched, this occurred to her: What I've always wanted is to celebrate my daughter in ways my mother could never celebrate me.

She'd gotten a letter from her mother during her final year in college, 1964. She kept it with the prints of those photos Celine had taken of her, and she knew it by heart. *In general*, it concluded, *I must ask you to be reasonable about your future and make a plan for yourself which is not adventuresome, not beyond your reach, one that you can follow through. Nothing you've told me in these twenty-one years has convinced me that you're altogether clear on the limitations of your abilities. All best, Celine.*

Now Alice was swinging Cam's arm. She started in on Sumin. Sumin looked at the treeline ahead. She and Cam would have to work together on this. There would be no coming up against Celine without coming up against her together.

Alice walked ahead of them, her head down.

Cam said quietly that she'd finished the portrait.

Sumin congratulated her. "Are you happy with it?" she asked.

Cam shrugged. "I'm not a very good artist," she said without a trace of self-pity. "I just know how to pose like one."

Alice had already turned around. She asked if they could go back now.

They headed back. "I was thinking," Sumin said. "I could suggest to Grady that he print it with the article." She watched their feet move down the path. She went on, "A kind of passing-of-the-torch angle." She looked at her daughter. "Of course, you could suggest it yourself," she added.

Cam stopped walking, her face was illuminated with surprise and delight. "No," she said. "It would be great if you did it," she said. "Really great."

Alice was ahead of them. "Come on," she said. "You guys are so slow."

They kept walking. Sumin felt better, and worse, than she had in months.

⤜⋙

He was an idiot. I was idiotic to have worried about his being otherwise. And now here I was stuck with him in my room as he went on reciting bits and pieces of my career, of my past, of Chinese history. All things that should've been put to rest long ago.

I tried getting him to talk about the child, but he didn't seem interested. Yet another reason she didn't belong anywhere near Sumin.

He asked about the series I had done of my mother. The Cultural Revolution photos.

How did he know about them? If Sumin had told him, she wouldn't have been able to resist pointing out that they were not Huying, but Sumin posing as Huying. Could Hsing Chiang have known about them?

His attention was nothing like the attention of an idiot. I said I'd torn those up. And now here he was embarrassing an old woman by resurrecting them.

Somebody had to, he said. He crossed his legs as if we had all the time in the world.

Sending him away seemed more foolish than staying, so I remained in my chair for what would come next.

*W*hen she got back, Sumin left a note on Grady's door: *I'm on the roof outside my room. Come up? The light's beautiful, and I'm a little sad.*

Alice came up behind her and asked what the note said.

Sumin suggested that Alice needed a bath. She told her to go ask Cam to give her one.

Alice frowned. "I don't have to take a bath, and," she said, "I found a tent."

"Good for you," Sumin said, walking past her.

Alice followed.

Upstairs, Sumin crawled out her open window onto the slanting roof.

"Cool," Alice said, coming out headfirst.

Sumin warned her there would be no

talking—it was thinking time—but she was pleased the girl was there.

She could make out the little bamboo bench at the crest of the hill in the back meadow. During the photo sessions, grass poked through its slats and spiderwebs hooked themselves across its corners, but it had been a wonderful place to sit to see the whole curve of the meadow down to the river.

Alice lasted longer than Sumin thought she would. She lay on her back, studying the sky, squinting every so often and furrowing her brow. Sumin wanted to ask what she was thinking about, but didn't want to break her own rule. She lay next to her, thinking about the luxury of enjoying something like this every day.

The evening gave way to night. Cam called them for dinner. Alice wrapped herself around Sumin's arm and said she wasn't hungry. Cam said she didn't care what she was, she had to eat dinner. Sumin said they'd both eat later. Silence from downstairs. Alice stayed wrapped around Sumin's arm.

She enjoyed an image of the three of them downstairs, unable to conceive of dinner without Sumin to make it, serve it and clean it up. She wasn't hungry either. She sat, listening for Grady.

Alice told her a little about her day. She said out of nowhere that Cam cried a lot. When Sumin asked why, Alice said Cam didn't know.

Sumin recalled the last summer at the cabin

when she had passed by Cam's room and seen her daughter standing in front of the mirror, picking at her eyebrows, saying over and over, *This is what I deserve; this is what I deserve*. What had been most disturbing was not the act of self-mutilation but the sense of power that seemed to come with it for Cam. Sumin had known, standing there watching her daughter, that the photos would not go on much longer.

When the stars began to appear Alice fell silent.

Soon her hand around Sumin's thumb relaxed, her breathing evened and Sumin got to eavesdrop on a child's sleep. She stared at the sky and tried not to push her thoughts in any particular direction.

The screen door downstairs swung open and banged shut. Cam's voice: "How do I know what they're doing?"

Her footsteps passed beneath.

A car door opened and shut. Footsteps returned. The screen door again. Nothing for a minute, then music. Was Grady still with Celine? She had no idea what time it was. Her back and rear were sore.

She sat up and shook Alice gently. "Come on," she said. "Time for bed."

Alice was barely awake, but wouldn't agree to getting into Sumin's bed. She wanted to sleep in the tent. Tomorrow night, Sumin promised. Then the floor, Alice negotiated sleepily.

Sumin made her a pallet in the corner with some quilts and towels, and she gave her a T-shirt to sleep in. Alice was back asleep the instant she lay down. She still had leaves in her hair. Sumin squatted next to her and picked them out.

She grabbed a blanket and went back out on the roof. She could hear Alice's breathing.

The music stopped and the lights downstairs went out. And then Grady was there, leaning out the window.

"Hey," he said. "Why are you sad?"

She motioned for him to be quiet and patted the roof next to her, and he dutifully and awkwardly climbed out to join her. She opened the blanket.

"So," he said, settling into place, "why are you sad?"

Even after five days here, his blue chambray shirt and his khakis, worn at the edges of the pocket, frayed at the back of the cuffs, smelled of unadulterated Grady—olive oil and sandalwood shaving cream.

"Ssh," she said. "Alice is sleeping on the floor."

"She is?" he said looking back into the dark room. "Why?"

"What time is it?" she asked.

"Almost one," he said. "I thought she was sleeping in your mother's room."

"She is, she was," Sumin said. "We were just hanging out and she got tired."

He looked worried. He wanted to know if she'd talked to Cam.

She shook her head. She started unbuttoning his shirt.

He let her maneuver his arms out of his sleeves. He asked for reassurances that she would talk to Cam; she gave them, and he lifted her hips to peel off her shorts. She felt weightless.

He piled her clothes somewhere and laid his weight along her length, wrapping the blanket back around them.

Her eyes were closed. "Take off your clothes," she said.

He did. They didn't make love. He curled himself around her, one arm under her neck, his other hand between her legs, cupping her. She listened to Alice's small noises.

It was exactly what she wanted, and she still couldn't keep herself from asking what he'd talked about with Celine. She asked if they'd talked about her and Alice.

He pressed his face into her neck and said no. "Mostly," he said, his lips moving against her skin, "we talked about the things you already know about from all your spying."

She put her hand on top of his, pressing his fingers against her. She told him she was sorry. She should've asked first. She told him that reading his words about the three of them, she could feel him physically.

She kissed him, and when she felt him returning the kiss, when she felt his fingers slip inside of her, she said, "Tell me what Celine said."

*H*er absence was impossible. I got out of bed, went downstairs and got the Toyo. Back in my room, I took it apart methodically. The assembly I had done millions of times, in reverse. It surrendered with ease. I laid its parts on the floor as if in a moat around the bed, the ground-glass focusing screen next to the infinity stops, next to the lens hood and board. I climbed back under the sheet and lay on my back, leaving room next to me if she returned during the night. Sumin's concern about Cam returned. I defended myself to no one. Around me, the organs of the camera floated like petals around a grave.

❧

*I*t was three in the morning. Sumin had been doing most of the talking. Grady asked her quiet questions, and she found herself talking and unable to steer the conversation to things she wanted to know.

He asked her about being a mother so young. He said that Cam had told him that Sumin always spoke of being a mother in the past tense. "I'm sorry," he said when he saw her face. She told him parenting was both something she had to do and something she was not quite capable of. He held her closer and told her she'd been a fine mother. She just had to learn how to listen better, how to need a little less from her daughter.

She felt herself getting hot. "It'll be better

with Alice," she said. She didn't say anything about what he'd be like as a father.

She knew this would be a good time to make her suggestion about Cam's portrait, but she didn't, and the moment passed.

They moved to the early shoots, the ones before Cam. They'd talked about them before, but going over it was like a reunion, and she'd never been able to resist that kind of sentiment.

She told of being a little girl in the cabin with Celine all those summers. She'd asked a lot of questions. Celine had finally had enough and had told her to stop trailing around behind her with nothing to do.

Grady made sympathetic listening noises. "What's horrible about that story is that she's always going on about the importance of questions. Tonight," he continued, "she argued that Eastern religions make more sense because they don't give you answers but questions. And, of course, she related it to her own work. All she does is tell people what they already know about her."

She waited to see if he would go on. She'd never felt completely knowledgeable about her mother, and knowledge was certainly what she needed now. She'd always thought Celine was the most beautiful woman she had ever seen, and it wasn't until Cam was almost twelve that Sumin, watching them both from the porch, had the feeling of having knocked into something and she'd found herself saying aloud, "*She* is more beautiful."

Now, with Alice beside her, Sumin felt more beautiful than she ever had.

The summer Cam was six, Sumin had needed to go back to the city early. She'd told Cam to write. Celine would help with the words. If she was really happy, she should write: *I am very happy here.* If she wasn't happy, she should write: *I am happy here.*

Sumin had been gone three days when she got a piece of paper with *I am happy here* written over and over again in circles around the paper. Only one of the sentences was in Celine's handwriting.

Sumin had called to find out what was going on. Cam was unhappy, she told Celine. You must not be treating her well.

Celine had reassured her: Cam was exaggerating. She was having a fine time. Just yesterday, she'd gone swimming.

"You *told* her?" Cam asked, when they were reunited. "You told her? I'll never tell you anything. Never."

How had her life become one betrayal traded for the next? She shut her eyes and attended the darkness behind her closed lids. She wanted to arrange her future. No: she wanted to rearrange her future. Alice. Alice would love her.

Grady was up on one elbow. "Are you sleeping?" he said.

She shook her head.

"Let's go in," he said. "You're tired."

"No," she said. "We'll wake her."

They were quiet.

"Well, I'm not going to sleep out here," Grady said.

"You'll make a great father," she said.

He didn't acknowledge the compliment. "You know," he said softly, "I've been thinking about Alice's mother." He paused. "I've been thinking that it might really be best for Alice to be with her own mother. We should talk about it more," he said.

Sumin felt tears coming. "You'd still make a great father," she said.

He squeezed her leg under the blanket. "Thanks," he said. "I'm still not sleeping out here," he added.

"Let's talk about Celine's mother," she said. She felt warmth go through his body. "We'll lie here, and you'll tell me what you know, and I'll tell you what I know, and then we'll go in." She hoped it was something he couldn't resist.

⌒

We just missed the famine of 1928. And the Terror. Ten years of slaughtering Communists. In 1931, the Japanese started their assault. I read about it, a small part of what must have really been happening, in the papers. And since my mother had never learned to read French, I would say, "Let me tell you the news from home."

And she'd nod, and say, "Yes, yes."

And I'd give her the gist. I'd read until she closed her eyes, and then I'd say, "That's it.

Nothing else," and I'd leave, giving her a light kiss as I went out. She was never interested in hearing the news from Europe. She didn't consider it her concern.

I should have made my mother and father more of my concern. I knew that. I could say that now. My understanding of what kind of daughter I was then would make me a better mother now. It was as important as physical strength. It would make up for the rest.

❧

UNTITLED

A SMALL GIRL straddles a rough pine bench. Her feet don't touch the dirt. She leans on one hand. Chin-length hair. The fingers on her other hand are splayed, as if she has just thrown dice. She is playing the Chinese version of jacks where pig-knuckle bones take the place of metal stars.

❧

They moved into Sumin's bedroom, shushing each other as they climbed into bed. Alice startled at the creaks, and they lay there for minutes, staring at the ceiling. One of the night-lights from Celine's shopping list lit Alice's corner. Sumin could make out the tangle of her hair across the pillowcase. From here, it looked like she was smiling.

They were, she realized, lying on top of the stolen pages. She reached down and pulled

237

the notes out. Grady didn't say anything, and they lay on their backs holding the papers in the dark.

She asked in a whisper where he'd gotten all the information.

Most of it, he told her, from scraps of the two autobiographies that Huying had been required to write: one upon her return to China, the other during her imprisonment. The rest from someone who'd known her housekeeper.

"She wrote those things down?" Sumin said, forgetting to whisper. "She wrote those things to be read by the people beating her?"

Grady told her that autobiographies like those were pretty routine at the time. Huying's first one had gone into her government file, but the second had been posted in both the prison yard and on her neighborhood news wall.

"But," Sumin went on, "she could've written what they wanted to hear." She realized she had no idea what that might have been.

Alice moaned and turned over onto her belly.

They turned on their sides and put their faces close, waiting for her breathing to deepen. This is like a family, she thought. This is what families do.

"She wasn't what you'd call a cooperative prisoner," Grady whispered.

She realized she'd been thinking of her grandmother as someone as passive as she would've been. This kind of bravery was foreign. She turned it over in her mind.

Grady went on, "She could've made things easier for herself. She might've survived. Lots of others did."

"She could've separated herself from Celine," she said. "Drawn a line."

Grady said, "Her daughter was more important."

He tucked his body closer. She pulled the covers back, and got up to put on her kimono. Celine had given it to her. Sumin liked it. It was cotton and had tiny tsunamis all over it.

"Where are you going?" he asked.

She pointed back outside.

"We're in bed," he said. He then muttered something she couldn't hear and got up, wrapping the blanket around himself.

On her way to the window, she knelt and rearranged Alice's blanket. Before standing up, she held the girl's feet in her hands. A Chinese nursery rhyme that Celine had sung with Cam went through her head.

A pig and a monkey do well not to wed,
And a lamb and a rat shouldn't share the
*   same bed.*
A rooster will run when it hears a dog
*   howl,*
And a horse can't endure the sight of a
*   cow.*
A snake and a tiger will bite, claw and
*   tear,*
And it's almost the same with a dragon
*   and hare.*

It had a typically Chinese title like "Song of the Twelve Bitter Enemies of the Zodiac."

Outside, they sat with their knees pulled up, a second blanket wrapped around both of them.

"I need a hat," Grady said.

"Hold your head in your hands," Sumin suggested.

"She didn't understand Celine's work," he said. "As far as I can tell, she thought the photos of Cam were in poor taste."

Sumin exhaled. She wished it were cold enough to see her breath.

Grady watched her. "But they mattered to Celine, and for Huying that was enough."

Things were turning that amazing shade of predawn blue.

"According to the housekeeper," he said, "she adored her daughter so much that she hid copies of the photos in her Little Red Book."

He seemed to think her reaction was insufficient.

He went on, "We're talking about a time when the smallest things had the largest consequences."

He leaned towards her. "One guy disappeared because of some bird's-eye-view snapshots he took from the top of a department store."

He waited for a moment. "He was charged with spying," he explained.

She had no response. Nothing came to mind. Oh? she thought. Wow? Why was she supposed to care?

Another woman had been jailed eight years for her Mozart collection.

"Oh," Sumin said. She wondered if there was room for her on Alice's pallet.

"Sumin," Grady said.

"Celine knew," he said. "She knew what her mother had to expect there."

Her head felt stupid. Here he was filling her in and all she wanted to do was stop listening.

"I didn't get it at first," he said. "Everyone talks about the nostalgia in the photos. But it isn't just that. It's nostalgia and hidden danger."

She said, "Celine always said she wasn't a political person; she said it was hard to make anybody change, and she wasn't the person to try."

She found herself wanting to say: They're just photographs. He was still talking.

"Being political isn't solely defined by how many protests you joined. All sorts of choices have political consequences. Whatever works best is what she'll swear by. Come on, this is a half-Chinese, half-French woman in a century of two world wars." He stretched his legs out in front of him, his feet sticking out from under the blanket. "You learn to become accommodating."

She did some calculating. His notes had said 'sixty-seven had been the worst year. She asked which of the photos from *One* had gotten Huying in trouble. Her mind filed through the ones she remembered: baby Cam in her crib with the ivy vine between her legs. The close-up of Cam at her breast. Celine had made Sumin cover with her hand the breast the baby searched for with her mouth.

Grady hadn't answered.

"What?" she said.

He told her it had been photos from another series, a series that Celine had ended up destroying. She felt as if she'd already known this, and her body was merely relaxing into the confirmation.

Specifically, one particular photo: Huying, shot from behind, in Western dress, leaning over a porcelain bust of Chairman Mao that lay shattered on the floor.

The breaking of Mao's icon was a crime of hideous proportions.

He doesn't know, she thought. He doesn't know it was me.

Celine had painted years onto her face with her makeup brushes. Cam had cooed from her playpen in the corner.

Her mother's hands had guided her into the composition. She'd loved the unfamiliar sensation of creating something out of nothing with her mother.

Whatever Celine and Cam had told him, it hadn't included that.

She looked at him. "When were they taken?" she asked.

"I guess during one of Celine's visits," he said. "They were interiors," he added.

Sumin nodded. He was assuming ignorance on her part. "What did she say about it?" she asked.

He gave her Celine's responses: Many people in China hadn't known what was happening. "Beans sizzling in the frying pan did not see the fire that made them jump," went the proverb. One always had to be circumspect. One didn't rush into things like here in America. She'd kept her wits about her and had done what had to be done. She'd quoted Lillian Hellman: she would not have cut her conscience to fit the year's fashions.

The only way was to "bend with the wind to survive the hurricane." Her mother had quoted the proverb to her on numerous occasions. She noted, for the first time, the extreme contradictions in Celine's pronouncements.

"How'd they find out about them?" she asked. Her legs ached, but she felt that if she moved, she'd tumble off the roof in pieces.

"Well," Grady said. He seemed reluctant to go on. "According to the housekeeper's friend, Celine gave copies to her mother. On one of her visits."

Sumin's head cleared. "Don't be nuts," she said.

Grady was aligning his feet with the edges of the shingles. "It might not have been stupidity," he said.

Neither of them said anything, the thought just dangling out there in the silence.

"What are you talking about?" Sumin asked.

He cleared his throat. "I'm saying it's hard to believe she didn't know what kind of consequences a gift like that could've had."

She thought she heard something inside. "Stop doing that," she said.

He looked up. "What?"

"With your feet."

He considered her.

"It's annoying," she said.

He pulled his feet back under the blanket. "It seems to make more sense that she sent them with that knowledge."

"That doesn't make anything like 'more sense,' " she said sharply. "Why would she do something like that?"

He didn't answer.

"Well?" she said. She was starting to get shrill. She remembered Alice and took a breath.

"Ego?" he said. "Need for approval?" He glanced out at the lightening sky. "You could understand that," he said.

She checked his expression. He wasn't mocking her. Celine had once said about Huying that she always seemed to slip around a corner just as you were coming up on her.

He waited for her to piece the implications together. As she did, she watched the creation she had made with her mother turn into destruction. The one connection between herself and her mother had been sliced neatly in half, and she turned the value of this information with respect to Alice over in her mind.

The sky had turned pink. There were birds.

He would want to know what she knew.

She knew that silence was a choice. Keeping her mouth shut was still an active choice with active consequences.

It was now within her power to turn away from these women and, just like that, swing from the defense to the prosecution.

She got up and went back inside.

Alice's bed was empty.

She got Grady, and they did a search. "Don't wake the others," Sumin warned him as they crept down the stairs.

They found her under the dining-room table. She was naked and asleep. Her bottom in the air. Her thumb was in her mouth. Sumin hadn't known that she sucked her thumb.

She got on her hands and knees and crawled under the table. Alice's face was puffy. Her breathing betrayed the after-effects of hard crying.

"I'll carry her," Grady said, bending over.

Sumin put a hand up. "You go to bed," she whispered. "We'll be fine."

He hestitated, but she didn't turn around, and after a minute more, he left.

She lay on her side next to the child. She traced the bumps and curves of her hand. Alice started sucking again. Her lips were chapped.

Sumin smoothed circles around Alice's back. Her skin was paler than it should've been after a week's sun. She imagined it as an undeveloped photo. Here's my photo, she thought. Here's my book. Here's my reward.

Saturday

Upon waking, still no Alice.

The camera pieces were fanned out around my bed like the tiny army surrounding Gulliver.

I collapsed and expanded the bellows, slid the focusing scale up and back, pressed my little finger into the holes for the lens-hood. I started to reassemble it, but there seemed no reason to do so. I put all the pieces loose into a traveling bag, as if they were children's toys. Then I stood around my room stupidly. I took a bath.

I was supposed to be helping Sumin with the dinner preparations. Tonight we'd celebrate birthdays and Cam would unveil her gift.

Sumin said she didn't need my help, and my tired body thanked her.

How would this body meet the demands of a child?

Hot, hot water, the steam dragon's breath filling the room. My body submerged, my eyes on the window at the foot of the tub. A pine bough through the glass. Beyond that, the tip of the far hill. A horse at the crest.

Behind the horse, my mother and father and

all the accompanying memories. All I could do was give in to the harmless ones and try to refuse the ones with teeth.

Kitchen sounds came up through the open window. Grady and Sumin. I listened for the child's voice. Where had she spent the night? How had I grown so accustomed to her in such a short period?

I was sweating. My hands were puckering beneath the water. I took a washcloth and laid it over my face, giving in to the heat.

The spring fair was the time for young women of good families to come with their maidservants, show off clothes and jewels and attract the glances of men. It was where my father first saw my mother. On the second day, he'd had the Western gall to slip her a letter wrapped in one of his English handkerchiefs.

Years later she told me that on that day the odor of France had been good to her. The medicine, the wool of his custom-made suits, and the almond of his French milled soap.

He told me that the first time he'd seen her, he'd been coming off a three-day shift at the hospital, and that seeing her face had been the equivalent of a full night's sleep.

Someone knocked. I pulled the washcloth from my face. *"Wei?"* I said, forgetting which world I was in.

Alice opened the door. "Speak English," she said.

"I was thinking of my parents," I said.

"What about them?" she said. She swung the door back and forth between her hands.

I cast around. I told her of my mother's battle against her family's resistance to the marriage. They'd locked her in her room; she'd kicked a hole in the door. She'd stopped eating and stopped praying to the ancestors. She'd listed what she would do to shame the family: never marry, run away, join the Revolutionary League.

Alice moved on to the towel bar. She flipped the edges of towels between her hands. "Those are very dumb parents," she said.

"I suppose," I said, closing my eyes.

"They should let her do what she wants," she added. She was at the sink, playing with the tap water.

"Where were you last night?" I asked.

She didn't answer. She let water pour over the back of her hand.

"I missed you," I said.

She nodded. "Uh-huh," she said.

"Were you in Cam's room?" I asked.

She turned off the water and wiped her hands on her shorts. "I'd rather be by myself," she said, apropos of nothing. *"Wo ziji lai,"* she added, and then she was gone.

It was the first Chinese I'd heard her direct towards one of us: I'll take care of it myself.

It wasn't the philosophy. It was her tone. The resignation, the sadness, her sense that this was her lot. Like the three-legged dog who looks at you with *Okay, fine, I can do this* in his eyes.

So even before the sounds of her steps had disappeared, I had decided. She'd said she wanted her mother to come here. She'd said this was what her mother wanted as well. This was what I would give them both.

~

*A*lice kept coming and going from the kitchen. She seemed preoccupied, and wouldn't answer their questions about why she had gone downstairs the night before. She seemed surprised to hear she hadn't been dressed.

Grady finally got to his point. He hadn't been able to get his hands on copies of the photos in question. If he didn't have them, he probably didn't have an article.

So this was not a retrospective celebration of Celine's work, was it? Sumin asked. No, Grady said. And it never had been? No, Grady said. It never had been.

"So what," Sumin said sarcastically, "an investigative exposé? Should I call you Geraldo?" She asked how long this article had been in the works. Was it the reason he had gotten interested in her in the first place?

His face made her instantly sorry for her cruelty.

He said that she knew better than that. Then he went on to the real question: Did she know of anyone with copies of the photographs?

"Can I sleep in the tent tonight?" Alice asked.

Sumin knew she was taking too long to answer him.

"Hello?" Alice said.

Sumin forced concentration. "We'll talk about it later," she said.

Alice frowned. "You're not my mother," she said.

"Then what are you asking me for?" Sumin snapped.

Alice left the room muttering to herself. Sumin went after her. Grady followed as well.

She took Alice by the shoulders. "I'm sorry," she said. "Now tell me what you want."

"Never mind," Alice said. She said she was going outside.

Sumin said she could sleep in the tent.

Grady repeated his question.

Alice perked up a little. "Outside, right?" she said.

"Yes," Sumin said. "Outside." She slid her hands down to the girl's. "Okay?"

"Sumin," Grady said.

She tried to get her mind around various consequences. "Grady, please," she said. "I can't worry about you right now."

He apologized. She had hurt him, she knew. Poor you, she thought, no article. Poor me, no life.

❧

*S*umin was in a particularly horrible mood. I mentioned that hopblossoms were especially good in soup, and she threw her dish towel and said, "You want to make the dinner? Go ahead."

251

I'd always had a distrust of group activities. It made no sense to have two queens in one hive.

But having reached my decision made me calmer. I apologized and backed away. This seemed to annoy her more.

I sat next to Alice at the kitchen table and watched my daughter work. She was mixing dough for the *jiao tze*. It should've been done the night before. I kept myself from saying anything. Her shoulders rolled with the movements of her arms. There was a kind of beauty to it. Her back was straight. It wasn't annoyance, exactly. There was something else. Something I could see, right there in her spine.

Again I was touched, this time by my version of Sumin.

Alice was drawing pictures of tents with flower beds around them. I allowed myself the imagined scene of revealing my decision to her.

"In the Shanghai house," I said, to either of them, "the cook sliced the vegetables with his fingernail." I raised a pinky, but neither of them looked. "When we moved to Paris and the cook there used a knife, I made fun of him."

Sumin's hands kept working. She said, "What were your birthdays like when you were a kid?"

There had been the camera, but then a string of presents that served only as indications of how poorly my parents knew me.

Without interrupting her drawing, Alice said, "I'll be seven next." She stopped her marker in mid-air. "When is my birthday?"

Both women were at a loss. I knew she had been born in the Year of the Rat, but the month and day escaped me.

She didn't seem to mind. "I think it must be soon," she said, stepping back to survey her work.

"Celine?" Sumin prompted.

"Lantern riddles," I said, pulling myself from Paris and back into China. "Paper lanterns with riddles in verse painted on them. The person who guessed the most answers won the prize."

She ran the water to rinse her hands. She wiped them on the sides of her apron and faced her next task, the filling. "I thought that was a festival tradition," she said.

She surprised me. "Yes," I said, "but it was a favorite of mine so my mother allowed it to be repeated for birthdays. The condition was I had to let the other girls win. The full-Chinese girls."

Sumin's butcher knife ceased chopping. "That's sort of Dickensian, don't you think?"

"It wasn't anything of the kind," I said. "It just was."

"*I'm* full Chinese," Alice said.

Yes, I thought, you are.

Sumin went back to chopping. Upstairs there was a crash, and we heard Cam swear.

"My mother did what she had to do," I said, "and instructed me to do the same. You bend with the hurricane to survive the storm."

"I need to call my mother," Alice said.

Sumin didn't answer, and again I was struck

with the sense of something other than annoyance in the air. The sound of the knife against the cutting board filled the room.

"We couldn't all have the luxury of a childhood like yours," I finally said.

She was making me anxious. I stood and said, "You'll never understand how much I sacrificed raising you."

Alice had put her markers away. "I have to call my mother," she said.

Sumin ripped the ground pork from its package and broke it into pieces over a big bowl. "Not now, Alice," she said.

I went on. "If I dwelt on shortcomings, it doesn't mean I overlooked the good points entirely. It means I believed it beneficial to hear the negative first and loudest."

Her hands were trembling. She scooped the chopped scallions into them.

"Is it my fault you've been able to create nothing but disorder in your life?" I asked.

Sumin started to defend herself, then stopped.

Alice raised her markers above her head and let them drop. We both stared at her. "I need to call my mother," she said.

I stood up. "Yes, you do," I said. "Come. I need to talk to her, too."

Sumin glanced up.

I took Alice's hand in mine. "You won't believe me," I said to Sumin, "but it would be my greatest joy if you could accomplish something more than the bits and pieces you've cobbled together."

I started for the other room, infuriated at how slowly I had to move. Alice tugged at me.

"My mother hated if I cried during times of celebration," I said. "It was not good to show sorrow before sorrow came."

Sumin wiped her eyes with the back of her hand. It was flecked with pork.

"I'm sure your mother would have been very proud," she said.

The comment didn't make sense, but her voice was nothing I'd heard out of her before. The serenity that my decision had brought was completely dissolved. I willed myself forward, step by step, feeling like the ailing mare circled by wolves.

❧

*S*umin lost herself in the dinner preparation. Much would have to be cooked at the last minute. The spicy string beans, birthday noodles, the *Ma Po Dofu*.

She allowed herself a break after stuffing the *jiao tze* and then started preparing the marinade for the steamed fish.

She mixed peanut oil, sesame oil, soy sauce, white wine, and shredded ginger in a shallow bowl, and eased the striped bass that Grady had picked up yesterday into the marinade, careful not to splash. She spooned sauce inside and over the bass.

It was supposed to be made with carp, but they were in Virginia. Carp, with its scaly armor, was associated with martial attributes, and because it swam upstream, was a sign of perseverance. She had no idea what was associated with bass. Probably the opposite of perseverance.

She was deep into preparing the centerpiece when Cam finally made an appearance. She breezed in and leaned over the table. "Cool," she said.

It was a large lotus flower and two buds made of peas, hard-boiled egg whites, peels of cucumber skin and slices of sausage.

"What is it?" Cam asked.

"What does it look like?" her mother said.

Cam picked up one of the impossibly thin slices of egg white. "How do you get the edges pink?" she asked.

Sumin took the slice back. "You dip the egg in food coloring before slicing it," she said.

Cam stretched. "Great," she said.

Since Cam had found out what Sumin wanted in terms of Alice, these were the kinds of conversations they had. Thin-ice conversations.

One day when Sumin had been ten or so, Celine had finally put her camera aside and spent an afternoon with her. She'd demonstrated what could be done with red double-blossomed garden balsam. She'd put a mixture of crushed petals and something else Sumin couldn't identify on Sumin's nails, wrapping them for the night with Saran Wrap, and the next morning Sumin's nails had been perfectly red. She'd spent the day moving her hands this way and that, performing unknowing imitations of Tang Dynasty aristocracy, Japanese dancers and other women with grace.

Cam went over to the counter and picked at the roasted beans cooling on a cookie tray.

Sumin's stomach was doing vague things. Had Grady talked to Cam about the photos?

"Where is everyone?" Sumin asked. She didn't want to get interrupted.

Cam shrugged. "The phone call was not a success. Alice is stocking her tent; Celine's packing, I think." She munched a bean. "She says you said she could sleep in the tent."

Sumin nodded. "Is that a problem?" she added carefully.

"No," Cam said, equally carefully. "No problem."

Sumin added the asparagus stem beneath the largest flower and tucked its end under the cucumber peels spread out to look like the leaf. The lotus flower, she thought. Summer fruitfulness. Purity and perfection. "Blah, blah, blah," she said.

"What?" Cam asked.

The rock pile of fortitude inside her was starting to shift and tumble. Things were not so bad, she thought. Cam was not so bad off, and neither was she. Guilt over not having mentioned Cam's portrait to Grady passed through her.

"Listen," she said. "We have to talk about Alice."

And they did. They went down to the honeysuckle caves, and Cam began, in a place that took Sumin by surprise. She said, "My happiness with Alice makes you unhappy."

Sumin said it didn't.

Cam nodded. "It does. And," she added, "it hurts my feelings."

The capacity to hurt Cam's feelings was something Sumin was sure she didn't have, but there was nothing disingenuous about her daughter's manner. Her daughter dug a small hole in the dirt with her finger.

"It doesn't make me unhappy. It just reminds me of what I didn't have."

Cam stopped digging, and jabbed her finger into the loosened dirt. "But it should make you happy regardless of what you did or didn't have. You're my mother. You should..." she faltered.

Exactly, Sumin thought. What should a mother do or be?

Cam went on. "I don't know...care." She brushed her fingers off. "Just *care*."

Sumin flicked a bug off her knee. "I care," she said, trying to sound less defensive than she felt.

Cam was shaking her head, and wouldn't look. "Sometimes," she said. "Sometimes I knew you cared." She pressed both hands flat into the red dirt. She looked up. "Remember that time I woke up in the middle of the night and you'd gone out while I was sleeping?"

Sumin shook her head.

"You waited till I was asleep, then you went out somewhere, I don't know where, and I woke up, and couldn't find you, and ended up calling that neighbor from across the hall. I was eight." Cam looked back at the ground. "Anyway, sometimes it was like that."

Sumin stared at her daughter. "I don't remember that," she said.

"I didn't think you would," Cam said.

They were both quiet for a moment, then Cam said, "So here's what I want for Alice. I want her to know all the time that I love her, that I'm listening to her, that I care about her." She didn't have to go on, but she did. "I don't want to be an unreliable mother."

Her whole life, Sumin had been waiting for intimacy like this with her daughter. She said, "It's just that sometimes I have this nostalgia for our life together."

"It was never just our life," Cam said. "Celine was always there."

Sumin sat up on her knees. "She wasn't *always* there." She said again that she was nostalgic for just the two of them.

Cam nodded. "The thing is, I'm not. Not at all."

How they went on from there was a mystery. But they talked more, about the photos and what Grady wanted. About the consequences of those photos. About the portrait. About Alice. About sharing her with each other or not having her at all. About what they wanted most and what they'd have to do to Celine to get it. It was the closest they'd been in years.

❧

Her mother hadn't been in.

Alice had grumbled that she was never at home, and I'd suggested that she find something to do that would make her feel better. She had gone outside.

I would need to make peace offerings to Cam and Sumin, but for now, I busied myself with Alice's present.

One of the only pieces of jade that had traveled with my mother. Chou Yuan had saved a small bundle of her belongings for me, sewn inside a cotton quilt: hair combs, the photo of her father and uncles, and this piece of jade. It was from a pendant her mother had given her when my mother had finally won her over about the marriage.

It was the fine apple green that Chinese prefer, so delicately carved in places that light shone through it. On it were carved the characters for the birth of a boy child, Double Happiness.

It had been my grandmother's peacemaking way of hoping that my mother's life would be happy, lucky and filled with boy children. A year later I'd been born.

When a boy was born, he was given a malachite ornament like a marshal's baton. A girl was given the curved tile normally used as the weight for the family spindle.

I'd give the jade to Alice tonight. She'd understand what it meant: that I wished for her what she deserved—the strength, the good fortune, the luck that our ancestors wished only for boys.

Outside, Alice. Toting various items: a sleeping bag, a backpack, a flashlight.

What to give Sumin and Cam? They who

would be hit hardest by my decision. Nothing came to mind. It had been years since I'd given Sumin a gift of any significance. And this had to do more than make her feel better about losing Alice. It also had to dissuade her from pursuing information about my mother. And Cam? How to keep from losing her?

I could think of nothing.

Alice passed by again. It seemed as if she were moving all her worldly possessions.

The jade was wrapped in tissue paper and nested in an embroidered box. In the card, I quoted Confucius:

In ancient times, men found the likeness of
*   all excellent qualities in jade.*
Bright as a brilliant rainbow—like
*   heaven. Exquisite and mysterious—*
*   like the earth.*
When struck, yielding a note, clear and
*   prolonged, yet terminating abruptly—*
*   like music.*
Its flaws not concealing its beauty; nor its
*   beauty its flaws—like loyalty.*
Standing out conspicuously in the symbols
*   of rank—like virtue.*
Esteemed by all under the sky—like the
*   path of truth and duty.*

❧

The lotus flower was set in the middle of the lazy Susan, its colors sharp against a glossy black plate. Sumin stepped back from the table to survey it. The blue fish bowls were the ones they always used; they'd survived all these years.

In the kitchen the food was sliced and chopped and sitting in ceramic bowls, the cooking chopsticks laid across them.

The high and low points of her conversation with her daughter ran through her. Where they'd ended up was so radically unprecedented that she willed herself to stop thinking about it, for fear of jinxing the whole thing.

The familiar feeling of setting herself up for a fall settled over her like a damp mist. But she knew that this evening there was something else: for once she was going into things with a head start. The weather reinforced the feeling; it was as cool as it had been all week. The wind blew through the house, and the sky was clear. She looked out the window over the sink. The sunset was unremarkable.

Tonight was some kind of last chance. "If you can't figure something out tonight," she said to the empty kitchen, "you might as well just give up." The trees beyond the porch shrugged their response, their limbs sluggish with summer leaves.

❧

was leaving tomorrow. I left out what I needed. Everything else I packed. I thought of whom I would need to contact about Alice's mother once I got back to Paris. The serenity was back. I was setting things right.

262

Alice in my doorway, her hair a mess, her clothes rumpled, a small tear at the hem of her shorts.

"Do you have any money?" she asked.

I laughed. "I happen to have millions," I said.

"Could I have some?" she asked.

I opened my wallet and handed it to her.

She took out a ten-dollar bill. "How much is this?" she said.

I told her.

She took another one. She seemed about to leave. I asked if I could tell her a story. She looked dubious. About my mother, I added. She hesitated, and I began, realizing at once that I was not catering the story to Alice, but to myself, with Alice as witness.

The last visit to my mother before she was imprisoned, we went for walks surrounded by street committee members.

When we were alone in the safety of her bedroom, I unpacked what I'd brought her. Her face told me they were not welcome. There was warm underwear. "Who am I to deserve this luxury?" she said loudly, directing her voice at the door.

There was money. Crisp one-hundred-dollar bills, and she took them, but only to fold them back into the envelope, leaving them on the table when she rose.

Alice glanced towards the open door. She fingered the folded bills. I went on.

I'd run through the rest of my belongings trying to think of something I could give that she would want, could keep. Finally, I took out the four-by-five prints from the series I'd taken of Sumin. I'd planned only to show them to her, but now it occurred to me that they were something she might want. She looked at them all, smiling at the sight of her old clothes. It was something, wasn't it, she said, how much her grandchild had come to resemble her old grandmother? Her eyes had begun to tear. It wasn't right, she said, for families to be this far away from each other. The guilt needled like an ulcer.

She spread the prints in front of her on the table. She said that the life she chose meant that she could not instill in me the traditional Chinese love for home. This, she said, was perhaps her largest regret.

At first she'd said, no, no, to my offer to keep them.

I'd just waited, letting my mother's pride push through me.

Later, when the consequences became clear, I could not get away from the image of her decision. She had chosen the most dangerous one, and all I had done was watch. Both her behavior and my own haunted me still.

Her eyes had scanned the room for the safest place to put it. She'd secreted it between the pages of her Little Red Book, and then turned to me and said, *"Hao, chih fan"*: Let's eat. We only held each other's stares for a moment longer than necessary before moving to the table.

Alice interrupted. "I know," she said.

"You know what?" I asked.

"I know about the photos," she said. "Grady and Sumin were talking about them." She stood up, and was gone.

The room grew cooler. Damage in various forms appeared. Without my reputation what was I? A scandal. Gossip. Forgotten.

Do not jump to conclusions, I told myself. There was no telling what they actually knew. There were no prints or negatives. There was no evidence. My heart would not slow.

September was two months away. The anniversary of her death. I would be back in Paris, safe in my little flat.

In September, the family sat under the moon to eat moon cakes and fruit, and absent family members were thought of with longing.

In my mother's garden, where we had sat one festival night the year before she died, I'd marveled at the camellias. I'd marveled at the Yulan. The iron statue of the stork in the shadow of her pine tree—emblems of longevity.

The warmth of her pride. I could feel it even now.

❧

*S*umin had just decided to go upstairs to shower and change when she heard sounds from the dining room. She peered around the door frame.

Cam was showing some red cards to Grady. Sumin couldn't see what they were.

"This is really great of you," Grady said.

Cam said she thought that Sumin had done

so much work on the dinner, that this would be a festive touch. She circled the table, placing a card on each bowl. And, she added, they'd been pretty honest with each other.

Grady said that he guessed the conversation had been harder for Sumin than it had for Cam.

Sumin was humiliated at Cam's sharing with Grady, and panicked that she had shared too much, but she still wanted to bury her face in her daughter's chest.

When Sumin had turned eighteen, her mother had given a party. Sumin had been the only teenager. She and her mother had sat across the room from each other. Celine had told anecdotes. The group had roared with laughter.

Then she'd gestured across the room and said, "Now you tell one."

The sunset had improved itself; the sky was lit in electric oranges, yellows and reds. She leaned over the kitchen sink and pressed her palm to the window, examining her hand against the fire outside.

❧

was dressed and ready before anyone else. I sat on the porch, drinking sherry. My mouth was dry, my stomach tight, as if my body was weighted and drugged.

I looked at the honeysuckle, to the crest of the back meadow, to the pond. Beautiful work had been made.

I was exhausted.

Whatever was to happen, I thought. Let it come. Alice would be safe.

Every day for the last twelve years since the photos had stopped, sunset backed me against memories of Cameron and our photos. It was when we'd accomplished our best work. The view camera's qualities had been suited for later in the day, and the film had had a long way of looking into the twilight. It made it palpable.

The success of my art had been largely due to my ability to conceal *why* Cameron had been an inspiration. The perceptive viewer allowed himself to be led to questions: Did she make pictures of what she liked? Of what she feared? Of what was beyond her attainment, that which she hoped to master?

The sky was already darker. I held my hands out against the sunset; they were hard to see in this light.

There would be no more photographs from me. The realization pushed me closer to death than any birthday ever had. But my limbs were lighter than they'd been in years. Just because something was beautiful did not mean it should be made a subject. The child had taught me this.

The photographs would last. Years ago it had been common for daguerreotypes to display no indication of their producer. Sometimes the signature of the artist was inscribed directly on the plate.

I took another sip of sherry. In overall terms, it was of no importance that there'd been no photos this week.

Sumin: most likely she knew nothing.

A boy in a baseball cap crossed the far hill with his sheepdog at his heel. The locals had always loved me. Our first caretaker had paid me his highest compliment: *She has the hand that puts the horse to sleep.*

Could I even imagine what she could do? How had this happened? After all those years of nothing from her?

And the answer came back to me like the horizon: You, Li Na. You did this to yourself.

The porch tilted and swam; I bent over and put my head between my knees. I ran through possible consequences: loss of my reputation, my position in the world. I had made the right decision about the child. Didn't I deserve something in exchange?

Extraordinary damage. And then, out of nowhere, taking me by surprise, relief. My head cleared. I sat up, and watched the end of the sunset.

❧

When they all sat down for dinner, Celine remarked that her mother had had an ink-brush painting of the lotus on her dining-room wall. A symbol of purity, she said.

Sumin's arms were loaded with the first course: cold chicken and vegetables refashioned into a colorful and arrogant rooster. Alice came behind her carrying the two dipping sauces. Sumin placed the chicken on the lazy Susan; Alice put the sauces on either side and said to Celine, "You always talk about your mother."

Everyone exchanged glances with everyone.

Celine said that little girls should pay attention to family stories, and then she turned to Cam and went on quietly about the old dining room.

Watching Celine chat about what Huying had and hadn't experienced sent an icy coolness down Sumin's back.

Celine told Grady that her mother had used silver chopsticks, believing the silver would turn black if it came in contact with poison.

Grady didn't respond.

"My mother had married a foreigner," Celine explained. "She thought about such things." She seemed chattier than normal; nervous.

"I'm sure she did," he said, and they left it at that.

No one said anything about the menu cards. Alice looked at hers and then put it under her bowl. She peered at the chicken. "I don't like that," she said.

"Yes, you do," Cam said. "It's chicken."

"Oh," Alice said. She sipped her juice.

"Don't eat it if you don't like it," Celine said.

Sumin had spent her childhood eating for breakfast what she hadn't finished at dinner.

"Don't listen to her," Cam said. "I make the eating rules here."

"I don't think so," Alice said, sliding out of her seat and under the table.

Sumin told her to get up and back into her seat.

Alice told her she could do what she wanted; it was a birthday.

Sumin said, "Not *your* birthday." She went on to say that Cam and Celine could do what they wanted.

Cam said that Sumin probably wasn't taking the right approach here. Celine wanted to know when Sumin had ever taken the right approach when it came to mothering. Grady was conspicuously silent. Cam seemed to be considering her grandmother's comment.

Sumin got up and headed back to the kitchen. Celine said something she couldn't make out, and everyone laughed.

In the kitchen she turned up the heat under the wok and threw in the shredded pork, and then added the scallions and some water. Steam hissed and billowed. More laughter from the dining room.

Were she and her daughter actually going to walk side by side?

She added the squares of bean curd. She piled a spoonful of white pepper at the bottom of the serving bowl and slipped everything from wok to bowl. She stuck a serving spoon into the dish and turned the stove down to low.

She stood with the bowl of steaming food in her hands. Did people really change? When she was little, she'd thought that people got better and better year after year. Life was slow improvement. Now she thought that people just got more accustomed to their own mistakes.

Cameron's beautiful hands were clasped under her chin. Alice was imitating her. They didn't seem to be listening to anyone. No matter what Sumin thought she was up to. This was my medicine.

Alice slid her eyes to me without moving her head. "What's wrong?" she asked.

"Nothing," I said. "I'm just looking at you."

It seemed as if her shoulders had become brown and smooth overnight. I resisted the impulse to cup them with my hands. I would make my announcement to the rest of them tonight. The child I would tell tomorrow, just the two of us, in our room.

"Well," Alice said, "I'm sleeping in the tent tonight."

The others were looking at us. Sumin had brought out the soup, the final course.

Alice groaned. "I hate soup," she said. "Can I be finished, please?" She kicked the leg of the table nearest her. Everything shook.

"Don't you want to stay for presents?" Cam asked.

I had to smile. Wonderful Cam. Always believed everyone would be thrilled with celebrations of Cam.

Alice kicked the table again. The surfaces of our soup trembled. "Actually," she said, "I don't think other people's birthdays are such a good idea."

"It's true," I said. "One's own is always more exciting."

She glared at me. Then waved her hand at all of us. "I'm making you all disappear," she said.

Cam sighed. "You can go," she said. And the child was gone.

We all stared at one another.

The tension of the dinner's nearing an end was transparent. Was my anxiety pointless?

Sumin had made Hainan coconut soup, served with Western soup spoons. I held mine up, struck by the oddness of the juxtaposition.

"We didn't have Chinese ones," Sumin said.

I tasted it. Cam was stirring hers around. She asked how much heavy cream was in it.

I remarked that she was right, that many believed that this soup was much too heavy for summer.

"I didn't say that," Cam said.

I took another sip, then put my spoon down and pushed the bowl away. I mentioned winter melon, which was rich in vitamins, cleaned the system, reduced swelling, stopped pain and made the skin smooth, soft and moist.

Grady nodded.

He was bovine. I'd wasted time worrying about him.

"I'm sure Sumin had reasons for choosing this soup," he said. He smiled at her.

Sumin nodded. "Mmm," she said. "You can also use it as paint thinner."

Cam said, "Did you want sons?"

Everyone looked at her. She pointed at me.

Geldings were the surer bet, I told her, but a good mare was better than the best gelding.

"So," Cam said, "your answer is…?"

I told her the answer had to do with whether the woman was ordinary or extraordinary.

Some women were extraordinary. Some women had strong character.

There was a silence. Grady looked at Sumin. He started to speak, but Sumin held out her hand. "Don't," she said, and then she turned to me. "Celine," she said. "What kind of character do you have?"

Everything I said seemed to elicit more deeply unrecognizable reactions.

I didn't know her well enough to know what she was capable of doing next.

Uncertainty ran through me like electricity.

She said, "What do you call those people so absorbed by one thing that everything else is up for sacrifice?"

I waited, and then said, as calmly as I could, "You always liked cocker spaniels. Perfect for you. They have frail nerves and feel constantly persecuted. 'Nobody loves me. Oh, nobody loves me.' Really, Sumin. You're getting tiresome."

"She didn't say 'me,' " Cam said. "She said 'everything.' "

The shock of Cam's defending her mother seeped through me. Just sit still, I thought. Tomorrow I would leave. I'd put this week behind me; things would be as they'd always been.

Finally Sumin stood up and started collecting the dirty dishes. She looked at Cam and said she thought it was probably time for the portrait. Her voice was precise and low.

❦

Sumin held the tray of dirty dishes over her head and tipped them into the sink. Almost all of them broke.

❦

No portrait yet, I said. First, a present for my daughter and my granddaughter. Both of them looked skeptical.

The idea had come to me during dinner. I'd make a photograph, I announced, of both of them. Neither of them had the reaction I'd expected.

Cam looked embarrassed, for me. For me!

I turned to Sumin. I couldn't read her face. Surely, this was the one thing she'd wanted longer than anything else in her life.

To my amazement, she laughed and said she didn't think so.

❦

Grady cornered Sumin in the kitchen making coffee. He wanted to know what was going on.

Sumin said it wasn't really about him.

"I suspect it is," he said.

She turned on the bean grinder and drowned him out.

He waited. "I suspect this has something to do with the photos," he said.

"As I said," she said. "It doesn't have much to do with you."

He was quiet. Outside, she could see the glow of Alice's flashlight through the tent.

He helped her load the coffee tray. "I think I should tell you that part of my article is going to include Alice."

"What does that mean?" she asked.

"Just what I said. That all this fighting that's gone on over Alice is, I'll be arguing, part of the larger picture."

Sumin surveyed him. She'd practically forgotten him already.

She took the tray from the counter and moved past him. "You do what you have to," she said.

❧

I stood by the window waiting for the end of the evening. Alice was moving around in her tent. Her shadows were unfocused against the yellow light. She seemed to be bent over something. A book? Her drawings?

Looking at her, even just her shadows, made me feel better about myself.

———

eline had an announcement. Celine was going to do the right thing. She was going to do all she could—and that, as they all knew, was quite a lot—to bring Alice's mother back to the States.

She knew they would be disappointed. She knew this wasn't what they wanted. But she could tell that this was right by how good it made her feel. This was the kind of act a good person took. If they didn't understand that now, they would someday.

Cam sank into her chair and folded and unfolded her napkin. She looked like she was about to cry.

Grady looked back and forth between Cam and Sumin.

Sumin had to call her daughter's name twice before Cam looked up. Sumin told her to get the portrait.

Cam didn't get up.

Sumin repeated herself.

Cam went upstairs and came back, the canvas in front of her body like a shield. She stood in front of her grandmother. She was crying now.

"Oh, for God's sake," Celine said, but she seemed genuinely unnerved at the sight of her granddaughter in tears.

Sumin kept her eye on Celine, but addressed

her daughter. "Show us the portrait," she said calmly.

Cam's fingers drummed the edges of the canvas. She had the look of a small girl trying very hard to master a difficult magician's trick.

"Stop crying," Sumin said. "It's going to be fine."

The painting ran from Cam's chin to her knees. She took a breath, glanced at her mother and flipped the canvas around.

It was Celine as a twelve-year-old, flanked by her father and mother. Sumin recognized the images from the photo Celine had of her arrival in Paris. She recognized Grady's hands and eyes in those of her grandfather's.

Bordering the canvas at haphazard angles were small versions of other photos. The covers of *One*, *Six* and *Twelve*. Cam and the farmer with the berries. Cam in her crib wrapped in a vine.

Sumin at two. The one from the photo book she'd given Cam. She hadn't known Cam had saved it.

In the top right corner, a woman from the back, in a Parisian suit, bending over a shattered bust.

Grady's stare on the side of her face was a distant heat, a fire miles away.

Celine's face was terrible.

Everyone had been silent too long. Cam lowered the portrait to rest on her feet. " 'Scrutinize the events of the past,' you used to say," Cam said to her grandmother.

Celine had both feet securely on the floor. Her fingers twitched against the arms of her chair like tiny timekeepers.

"It's a visual path," Cam said. She looked up. "You know. How you got from there to here."

"I understand what it is," Celine said. Her voice sounded as it always had.

"Sumin," Celine said.

Sumin looked across Grady.

Her mother's face was unreadable. "Sumin," she said again. "What do you think of what your daughter has done?"

Sumin continued to look. It seemed as if all three of them were waiting for her. Celine seemed disconcertingly calm. But slowly and with more ease than ever before, her mother's expression became clear to her: I kept you in my life, and this was my reward.

"I have the photos," Sumin said.

"Of course you do," her mother responded. "And you're proposing a trade: the photos for Alice." She looked back and forth between granddaughter and daughter. "You've joined forces," she said with a trace of sarcasm. "And left the poor mooncalf out of the whole thing." She smiled at Grady.

She stood and addressed Cam. "You know that the decision I came to is the right one; the one best for the child."

"You don't ever make decisions for anyone else's benefit," Cam said.

"You *know*," Celine said.

"If it's Alice you're concerned with," Sumin

said, her eardrums pounding, "then tell us to shove it. Tell us to go public with these photos and all of their implications."

Celine was shaking. She was making her way to the stairs. There was sweat on her upper lip.

Sumin followed. "Go ahead, Mother. Make your own trade: your reputation for what's 'best for the child.' Do the right thing."

Cam watched them, the portrait resting atop her feet. Grady got up.

Celine pulled herself onto the first step. She said, "You should both be ashamed of yourselves."

Sumin leaned on the bannister. What was she doing? Who would she be without being her mother's daughter?

Celine was halfway up the stairs. Her breathing was audible. And from one moment to the next, Sumin understood. She had, of course, never been more her mother's daughter.

She listened to her mother's laboring. From behind both of them, Cam said, "We should all be ashamed of ourselves."

Sunday

On the morning, we discovered, as we should've known we would, her note.

She had laid it across the pillow where her head had been. Its bottom edge was tucked into the sleeping bag. She said goodbye. She said not to worry. She said she didn't think she could stay there anymore.

There were spelling errors.

The three of us knelt around the empty sleeping bag. We took turns reading the note. We concentrated on looking everywhere but at one another.

Let's look for her, we said.

Let's find her, we said.

We'd find her, we said, on the one road leading away from the cabin. And we would. Practical Alice would certainly keep to the road.

Finally, from our corners, we raised our eyes. And in them we saw what we knew we would, what we had always known. Without Alice, it was just us. But also something else, something more, something we were just beginning to know: just us might be enough.

Acknowledgments

'm grateful to the following individuals for just the right kinds of help at just the right times: David Alexander, Cathleen Bell, Michael Davitt Bell, Kristin Carter-Sanborn, Cassandra Cleghorn, Peggy Diggs, Ed Epping, Ron Hansen, Richard Howard, John Hyde, Janet Turnbull Irving, Susan Jones, John Kleiner, Sandra Leong, Katherine Longstreth, Laura Mathews, Peter Matson, Maureen Murray, Paul Park, Marsha Recknagel, Caroline Reeves, Shawn Rosenheim, Geoff Sanborn and Scott Wong.

And I'm grateful to my family for all kinds of help at all kinds of times: James Connolly, Amy Glazer, Leonard and Zelda Glazer, Mitch Glazer, Sidney Glazer, Han Suyin, Kelly Lynch, Albert and Ida Shepard, and Yungmei Tang.

Finally, and most of all, thanks to my first and ultimate reader, my husband, Jim Shepard, who has taught me more about what it means to be a reader and a writer than I ever thought I would know.